FIC Sor
Sorrells, W
Fake ID

W9-APC-258

TRUTH IS, I DON'T KNOW MY NAME.

In Quincy, Illinois, I was Lynda Sue Greer. In Deer Park, Washington, I was Rose Ford. In Columbus, Ohio, I was Renice Preminger. There were a lot more names, one as bad as the next. I can't even remember them all. All I can say is that everywhere we go, I always end up getting stuck with these old-fashioned doofus hick names. Mom says it's a jinx, but I don't believe in jinxes.

Why all the names? See, Mom and I have been on the run for as long as I can remember. From what? I don't know. It's the one thing Mom would never talk to me about. Sex? Sure. Drugs? No problem. Boys? Easy. But not the reasons why we were running. That subject was off-limits. That and my father. I don't know who he was, or even what his name was.

But now everything's gone bad, and I only know one thing: I have only six days.

Six days to figure out who I really am.

• • •

NOBLESVILLE HS LIBRARY
NOBLESVILLE, IN 46060

OTHER BOOKS YOU MAY ENJOY:

Double Helix — Nancy Werlin

Gilda Joyce,
Psychic Investigator — Jennifer Allison

Haunted — Judith St. George

The Invisible Detective:
Double Life — Justin Richards

The Invisible Detective:
Shadow Beast — Justin Richards

The Sword That Cut
the Burning Grass — Dorothy & Thomas Hoobler

FAKE ID

HUNTED: BOOK ONE

FAKE ID

WALTER SORRELLS

SPEAK

SPEAK
Published by the Penguin Group

Penguin Group (USA) Inc., 345 Hudson Street, New York, New York 10014, U.S.A.
Penguin Group (Canada), 90 Eglinton Avenue East, Suite 700, Toronto, Ontario, Canada M4P 2Y3
(a division of Pearson Penguin Canada Inc.)
Penguin Books Ltd, 80 Strand, London WC2R 0RL, England
Penguin Ireland, 25 St Stephen's Green, Dublin 2, Ireland (a division of Penguin Books Ltd)
Penguin Group (Australia), 250 Camberwell Road, Camberwell, Victoria 3124, Australia
(a division of Pearson Australia Group Pty Ltd)
Penguin Books India Pvt Ltd, 11 Community Centre, Panchsheel Park, New Delhi - 110 017, India
Penguin Group (NZ), Cnr Airborne and Rosedale Roads, Albany, Auckland 1310, New Zealand
(a division of Pearson New Zealand Ltd)
Penguin Books (South Africa) (Pty) Ltd, 24 Sturdee Avenue,
Rosebank, Johannesburg 2196, South Africa

Registered Offices: Penguin Books Ltd, 80 Strand, London WC2R 0RL, England

First published in the United States of America by Dutton Children's Books,
a division of Penguin Young Readers Group, 2005
This Sleuth edition published by Speak, an imprint of Penguin Group (USA) Inc., 2007

10 9 8 7 6 5 4 3 2 1

Copyright © Walter Sorrells, 2005
All rights reserved

THE LIBRARY OF CONGRESS HAS CATALOGED THE DUTTON EDITION AS FOLLOWS:
Sorrells, Walter.
Fake ID: a novel / by Walter Sorrells.—1st ed.
p.   cm.   Summary: After a lifetime of moving and assuming new identities, sixteen-year-old
Chass begins to piece together the disturbing past that haunts her and her mother and which
involves a mysterious tape, a deceased popular singer, and the secrets of several people in a
small Alabama town.
ISBN 0-525-47514-1
[1. Murder—Fiction. 2. Mothers and daughters—Fiction. 3. Secrets—Fiction. 4. Identity—
Fiction. 5. Musicians—Fiction. 6. Alabama—Fiction. 7. Mystery and detective stores.] I. Title.
PZ7.S7216Fak   2005   [Fic]—dc22   2004021578

Speak Sleuth ISBN 978-0-14-240762-2

Printed in the United States of America

Designed by Gloria Cheng

Except in the United States of America, this book is sold subject to the condition that
it shall not, by way of trade or otherwise, be lent, re-sold, hired out, or otherwise
circulated without the publisher's prior consent in any form of binding or cover
other than that in which it is published and without a similar condition
including this condition being imposed on the subsequent purchaser.

The publisher does not have any control over and does not assume any
responsibility for author or third-party Web sites or their content.

31111000054591

To Liliana, my first reader

FAKE ID

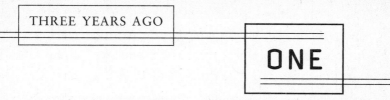

ONE

MOM IS WEIRD about music. Like she won't listen to it. I mean, *at all*. She says music is bad luck.

And given how things worked out, maybe she's right.

Anyway, the reason I mention this is that I knew she was in a good mood as we drove into our new town for the first time because she let me turn on the radio and sing. Even though the radio only received AM and we were in some Podunk part of Alabama and all they had on the air was corny old country music—I didn't care, because I love to sing *that* much. We'd been driving for like twelve hours straight, leaving Columbus, Ohio, and heading for this little town in Alabama that was going to be our new home. We were tired, we were nervous, we were hot and sweaty because the air conditioner in Mom's old beater Volvo wasn't working. But it was okay because Mom was happy. When Mom's happy, the whole world's happy.

After about five minutes of singing—just as Mom started getting all weird and jumpy and antsy—the sign at the edge of our new town came up on the side of the road. WELCOME TO HIGH HOPES, ALABAMA, THE TOWN WHERE EVERYBODY'S SMILIN'! Mom said, "I have a good feeling about our new home, Bug." She calls me Bug, which is short for June Bug, which is not my real name, as you might imagine. "Let's don't jinx it."

She turned off the radio.

I looked out the window. The town didn't amount to much. It was surrounded by wide green fields, the spring crops just peeking up from the red dirt. On the edge of town, there was a Feed and Seed store with Purina signs over the long wooden porch, and tractors and shiny pickup trucks parked around it. Then there was a video store and a Chick-fil-A and a restaurant called Honcho's Fine Food, then some nice old *Gone-with-the-Wind*-looking houses with white columns. Then we were on the main drag of the town, a street about ten blocks long, lined with old two-story brick buildings. Unlike most of the dinky little hick towns we'd just driven through, all the downtown businesses in High Hopes looked prosperous, and the place seemed full of life. The cars parked on the street were new, and the people were well dressed and attractive, walking around with a sense of purpose. It wasn't what I'd expected from Alabama. I was imagining shacks and hillbillies with banjos, I guess.

A big county courthouse with a gold dome sat in the middle of the town square. A Confederate soldier made of limestone stood on a pedestal out front, trying his best to look all heroic and everything while the pigeons crapped on his big hat.

The public library was across the street from the Confederate soldier. We pulled up and parked, then went inside and stood in the lobby for a minute, luxuriating in the air-conditioning.

"Well?" Mom said finally. "Ready?"

I nodded. We had a ritual, how we came into a new town. For reasons I'll get into later, we moved around a lot and so we had this whole routine, this tried-and-true procedure that we went through every time we came to a new town.

The way it started was like this:

We walked back to the fiction section of the library and into an aisle with a little sign tacked onto it that said F THROUGH H. Mom always started in the *F*'s. I don't know why, that's just how it was done. I walked down to the far end of the aisle, then turned around. Mom was still standing at the other end of the row of shelves, looking at me.

"Go ahead," I said.

Mom closed her eyes, then began walking slowly, slowly, slowly down the aisle, one finger dragging across the spines of the books on the shelf next to her. It made a soft *blip blip blip blip* sound as her fingernail clicked across the spine of each book. She had a dreamy expression on her face, smiling a little, like she was imagining something really good happening to us for a change.

After a minute I said, "Stop."

She halted immediately, the vague smile hanging there on her lips. Then after a couple seconds, she opened her eyes, looked over to see what book her finger was resting on. "*The Jewel of Castle Ravenwood,*" she read off the spine of the book, "by Charlotta Fotheringbroke."

"Oh, God," I said. "Tell me that's not one of those bodice rippers."

Mom grinned mischievously, pulled the book off the shelf, held it up for me to see.

"You have *got* to be kidding me, Mom," I said. There he was on the cover of the book—Fabio, in all his glory, with his big canned-ham pecs and his girl hair, sweeping some bosomy chick in a froofy dress off her feet.

"No, please!" I wheedled. "Do it again."

"Rules are rules," Mom said. "No do-overs."

She opened the book and started reading in this real bad, fake English accent. "Chapter one: 'As the north wind howled eerily through the forbidding black stone walls of Castle Ravenwood, the young girl sank to her knees and began to moan. "Please, my liege, do not make me go!" The tall, handsome young duke looked down at her, his face absent of pity. "I have made my command, Chastity Pureheart. You are forever banished from this land!"'"

Mom stopped reading, closed the book, and started laughing her ass off. Behind her a bunch of old dudes reading newspapers looked up at her, all disapproving, like she'd just farted or something.

"No," I said. "Absolutely not. You have to go again."

"Rules are rules," she said brightly. "The first female name in the book."

"Chastity *Pureheart*?" I said. "No way!"

"Come on, Bugaboo," she said. "You know good and well that if you don't do it, we're totally jinxed."

"Nope," I said.

"I let you listen to the music," she said. "That was strictly against protocol. So we have no choice."

"Mom!"

She just smiled. "See you back at the car, Bugster." Then she turned and walked off with her happy, hip-swinging walk. As she walked out the door, I could see all the old retired men sitting around reading their newspapers. They looked up at Mom for the second time and watched her with their mouths half open. Mom's hips had that kind of effect on guys, even really old ones.

I stood there for about five minutes, hating my mom, hating my life, hating what I was about to do. Problem was, we had a way of doing things—a routine, a plan, a ritual, whatever you want to call it—and even though I wanted to strangle my mother, I felt loyal to the ritual. If we didn't have the ritual, what did we have? Nothing, that's what. Pathetic but true. We had absolutely, totally nada.

Finally I took a deep breath, walked up to the front desk of the library, and said, "Hi, I just moved to town and I want to apply for a library card."

"Sure, darling." The librarian was a sort of swishy-looking guy with very neat hair and very neat polyester clothes and a nice expression on his face. He had the drippiest southern accent I'd ever heard in my life. "What's your name?"

I smiled as hard as I could manage under the circumstances, tried to look all sincere and everything. Then I said, "My name's Chastity Pureheart."

And that's how it starts.

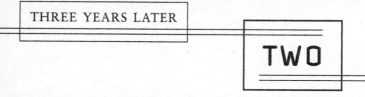

THREE YEARS LATER

TWO

GO AHEAD. YOU can call me Chastity Pureheart, I guess. Whatever. I go by Chass, which I actually don't mind. It's not my real name obviously, but it'll have to do.

Truth is, I don't know my name.

In Quincy, Illinois, I was Lynda Sue Greer. In Deer Park, Washington, I was Rose Ford. In Columbus, Ohio, I was Renice Preminger. There were a lot more names, one as bad as the next. I can't even remember them all. All I can say is that everywhere we go, I always end up getting stuck with these old-fashioned doofus hick names. Mom says it's a jinx, but I don't believe in jinxes.

Why all the names? See, Mom and I have been on the run for as long as I can remember. From what? I don't know. It's the one thing Mom would never talk to me about. Sex? Sure. Drugs? No problem. Boys? Easy. But not the reasons why we were running. That subject was off-limits. That and my father. I don't know who he was, or even what his name was.

But now everything's gone bad, and I only know one thing: I have only six days.

Six days to figure out who I really am.

THREE

MY MOTHER DISAPPEARED on the night of my six-teenth birthday. Because I'm such a social outcast, it was a pretty pitiful little party. Just me and Mom and my pla-tonic friend Ben Purvis. Ben had brought over this huge box with a giant red bow on it.

"Come on! Open it!" Mom said. She was all smiling and winking and excited about the big red bow because she wants Ben to be my boyfriend. Which he totally is not.

"Let's eat first," I said glumly. "I can open it later."

"Come on, Chass!" Mom said.

But I wouldn't back down. So the huge box sat unopened on the other side of the room while we ate dinner with my mom in our crummy little apartment, and I kept sneaking glances at it and feeling all queasy. Because I knew what was in the box.

Mom kept making jokes about the box and about Ben. She even referred to him as my "boyfriend." Which I hate. He's my best friend in the world, but like I say, he's not my boyfriend. I just don't think of him that way. He's really smart and funny, and he plays guitar and sings— but he's not my type. Not in the boyfriend way. Ben is like six foot two, but he's only about 150 pounds, and he always wears army pants and T-shirts with the names of all these death metal bands on them, and half the time you suspect he didn't wash his hair the night before.

Whereas, I don't know why, but I always fall for the popular-jock-student-council-president-most-likely-to-succeed-type guys. And, of course, they don't give a damn about me.

Anyway my mom kept hinting around about the big box, and I kept making excuses. So Mom finally got out the saggy, miserable-looking chocolate cake and everything, and I blew out the candles, and she got all dewey eyed—"Oh, my baby's just turned sweet sixteen!" and all that junk—and I was just stalling like crazy because I didn't want to open that box.

"Presents, Chass! Presents!" Mom brought in a present that was wrapped in her usual careless, slapdash way and put it on the table, and I unwrapped it and pretended that I was really happy she'd given me a book of poems by Sylvia Plath, this chick who killed herself a long time ago.

"Thanks, Mom," I said. "But don't blame me if I go out and drown myself after I read all this stuff."

She looked all hurt, and I told her I was just kidding.

"Now Ben's present," Mom said.

"Uh . . ." I tried to think of some kind of excuse, but I came up totally dry.

Mom gave me a funny look. And Ben's staring at me with this sweet puppy dog face. I was like, *aw man, do I really have to?* But I couldn't avoid it—not without hurting Ben's feelings.

So I got up and trudged across the room and brought the big box back and started tearing off the wrapping, and Mom had to go into the kitchen and bring out a butcher knife because I couldn't get the huge red ribbon untied and it turned into this huge production and I was like, *God, just kill me now.* Because, like I say, I knew what was coming. The present and the whole big ugly scene that would follow.

So I finally got the wrapping off, and there was a brand-new box that said TAKAMINE on the outside. My

14

heart was going *gizh gizh gizh gizh* really fast. "No. This isn't right," I said.

Mom was looking at me with a curious expression on her face. I guess she didn't know what a Takamine was.

A little wrinkle appeared in the middle of Ben's forehead, right above the bridge of his nose.

"I mean really, dude, this is too much," I said. I wasn't just saying it. It *was* too much. "You shouldn't have."

Ben grinned. "You kept looking at that one in the pawnshop," he said. "But I figured, why get a used one, right? So I went over to Atlanta and got this one. Had to special order it straight from the factory."

I was like *damn damn damn damn damn*. I could feel my pulse knocking around in my temples, and this rushing sound was in my ears. Because I knew how hard Ben had worked for this, and I knew there was no way I could keep it.

Mom kept staring at the box. "What is it, Chass?" she said. Still all excited. "The suspense is killing me!"

So I slowly opened the box, and there was the thing I wanted most in the whole wide world. It was a Takamine acoustic guitar. And not one of the bottom-of-the-barrel models. This one had pearl inlay on the neck and an ebony fingerboard, mahogany back and sides. It was so shiny I could see my face reflected in it. Snub nose, blond hair, a slightly apprehensive look in my blue eyes. Apprehensive, because I knew it had cost about a grand. Which meant that Ben had been saving every nickel he'd made cleaning out the fryers at Honcho's Fine Foods for the past six months to pay for it.

I couldn't even look at my mother's face.

Ben was grinning, showing all his big square teeth. "This one has the piezoelectric pickup and everything," he said. "And listen to the tone! Play it and listen!"

Finally I looked at my mom's face. She looked like somebody had kicked her.

"No, Ben, I'm sorry," Mom said, her voice coming out all cool and distant. "But this is out of the question."

He just blinked and looked at her.

"This is way too expensive," Mom said. "You'll have to take it back. Besides, Chass doesn't even know how to play."

"Sure, she does," Ben said. He was still smiling, no idea what he'd just walked into. "What do you think she does every day, coming over to my house? She just pretends to be friends with me so she can play my guitar. She practices like two hours every day over at my house."

Mom's gaze shifted from the guitar to my face.

Good old Ben. Couldn't keep his mouth shut. He just kept digging me in deeper: "I started teaching her back in ninth grade, Mrs. Pureheart. By the end of the year she was better than me. Then my dad taught her, and now she's better than him too. You got to hear her! She totally rocks!" He picked up the guitar and jammed it into my hands. It felt like electricity was running through my whole body. I couldn't believe I was holding it. It was so perfect and beautiful I wanted to cry.

Mom's face was white. She looked at me with this strange expression, like I'd just stabbed her in the back. Betrayal. That was what I saw in her eyes.

Music is bad luck. The ultimate jinx. For me to play music, to *devote* myself to it—it was like I was spitting in her face.

She was staring at me, her eyes all hollow and everything, and I don't know what came over me, but I just started playing. I mean, I'd been drooling over all these guitars for a couple years now, guitars that weren't half as good as this one. And to have it sitting there in my hand? And not play it? I just couldn't do it.

So I started playing this song "Am I Living It Right?" by my hero John Mayer. Some people think John Mayer is kind of bubblegum, but what they don't realize is he's a totally kick-ass guitar player. So the song is a real knuckle buster. But the guitar was so nice, the action so silky, that the song just came reeling out of my fingers like it was the easiest thing in the world.

And Mom closed her eyes and stood there stock-still while I played, her head cocked to the side like she was hearing music for the first time in her life. I played all the way through the song, playing the tricky little bridge like I'd written it myself, then singing the last verse. And then when I was done and the sound of the guitar and my voice had died away, Mom opened her eyes, and the tears started running down her face. Just spilling, like a hose.

"I can take it back," Ben said. "I'm sorry, I don't know what's going on here, but I can take it back."

"You want me to give it back, Mom? Huh? Huh, Mom?" I said. I was staring bullets at her. And suddenly this strange feeling came over me. I don't know why it hit me just then, but I had this totally overwhelming feeling that I had come to a place where nothing would ever be the same. Why then? I don't know. All I was sure of was that I had made a choice I couldn't turn back from. "Well, I'm not gonna give it back. It's *mine*."

She didn't say a word.

Ben reached for the guitar, but I held on to it like I was drowning and this was the only thing that would keep me from going under. Ben's eyes widened, and he let go.

"You know what, Mom?" I said. "I won the talent show at school last month. All the kids over there hate me, but they still voted me the most talented person in the whole school. That's how good I am. And I couldn't even tell you."

Mom sort of waggled her head, like she was trying to dislodge something that was stuck in her brain.

"How screwed up is that, Mom? Huh?"

"Watch your tone of voice, young lady," she snapped. But then the anger sort of drained out of her, and she just looked old and used up. I'd seen her look depressed, scared, worried, freaked-out—all kind of stuff. But never like that. Never *old*. Then she turned around and walked out of the room, slammed the door. I heard the car start up, the tires screech, and then she tore off down the road.

"I better go," Ben said.

"If you go right now, dude, I will totally *kill* you," I said.

Ben gave me this queasy smile, and then we sat there for a minute, and the room was dead quiet. Finally Ben cleared his throat, and then he went, "So . . . what was this all about?"

I shrugged. "Mom's got this thing about music. She doesn't like music in the house. Actually she doesn't like music at all."

Ben looked at me like I was crazy.

"Hey, believe me, I know," I said.

"Is it like some religious thing?"

I shook my head. "She just doesn't like music." I wasn't going to get into how she thought it was bad luck.

"Anybody ever tell you your mom is kinda nuts?" he said.

"You have no idea," I said. It came out sort of bitter sounding—which I didn't mean it to. Then I said, "Did you bring your guitar?"

He nodded. "It's in the Batmobile." Ben's a year older than me, so he can drive at night. He owns this huge crappy black Lincoln from the '70s that breaks down all the time. We call it the Batmobile.

"Go get it."

"I better not."

My voice got a little hard. "Go get it."

One of the many things I like about Ben is that he pretty much does anything I ask him to. He went to his car, came back with his old pawnshop Washburn guitar. We sang Elvis, we sang John Mayer (did I mention he's my hero and he totally kicks ass), we sang Beatles, we sang Ryan Adams, we sang hymns—everything I could think of. We even sang "Oops I Did It Again," which is like the worst song in history. We played music until my fingers were blistered and my voice was ragged. Then we played some more. I had never sung out loud in my house, not in my whole life, and it felt great. It felt like something was busting out of my chest, something that had been all tamped down and stepped on for my whole life. It felt almost as good as having a name.

But then, after a certain point, I started getting this nervous tingle. Three hours had gone by, and Mom was still not home. That wasn't like her. But we kept playing, even though Ben was tired and was supposed to have been home at midnight. And eventually, at a certain point, I went from nervous to flat-out scared. But I kept playing anyway. I was so mad at Mom that even though my fingers were killing me and Ben had stopped playing, I kept going out of pure spite, kept playing and playing.

Until finally I noticed that my fingers were bleeding, getting blood all over the neck of the guitar.

I looked at the clock. It was five past one in the morning. Still no Mom.

I wiped the blood off the neck of the guitar, set it down gently on the couch, and said, "I think I better call the police."

FOUR

SOMETIMES YOU WANT to do a thing because the other girls at school do it. Sometimes you want to do a thing because it pisses your mother off. Sometimes you want to do a thing because you've seen people doing it on TV and it seems all glamorous and cool. But sometimes you just want to do something because, bone deep, you know it's right.

It was that way the first time I touched Ben's guitar. I picked it up, and something in my fingers just knew what to do. I don't mean I already knew how to play or whatever. It was just that when I wrapped my fingers around the neck of his old Washburn, I knew: *This is where my hand is supposed to be*. It was like, *bing!* Like the elevator has stopped, and this is my floor, I'm getting off here.

When you've never known your real name, or who your father is, or where you're from, or what your grandma looks like, or what city you were born in—then knowing anything about who you really are is precious. I mean, I don't know much. But when I touched that guitar, I knew that I knew something. For the first time in my life, I *knew* something! I knew *this* was what I was supposed to do with my life.

Call it musical talent, if you want. I mean I've gone to a zillion school talent shows, watched all these kids making wreckage out of perfectly good songs, banging away on the piano or torturing some poor violin or whatever, and let's face it, most kids suck at playing music. That's a fact. But after playing Ben's guitar for like three or four months, I realized I had talent. I could see it in people's faces when they heard me play. I could feel it. But that's not the point. The point is that I knew I was built—right out of the box—to do this. It was something in my blood. It was something that came out of that dark hidden place where my true identity lay.

And that pissed me off. Because here I was, already in high school, and my mom had deprived me of this one little morsel of comfort, this one thing that I could have had as we drove around the country throwing away clothes and apartments and cars and friends and names. I could have had this one thing the whole time. And my mom stole it from me.

FIVE

"I JUST GOT a weird phone call, Chass," Ben's dad said, talking to me in the living room of Ben's house, the phone still in his hand.

"Weird how?" I said. My heart started beating fast.

I had been staying over at Ben's place for the past three days. It was three days since Mom had disappeared, three days since I had called the sheriff's office to file a missing persons report, three days of freaking out every time the phone rang.

NOBLESVILLE HS LIBRARY
NOBLESVILLE, IN 46060

Ben's dad, Addison Purvis, is like this old hippie who makes sculpture in this broken-down shop in his backyard, and everybody in town thinks he's strange. But I like him.

"There may be some news about your mother," Mr. Purvis said. "Maybe I better go over and see."

"Over where?"

But Ben's dad didn't say. He just walked out the front door and headed for the car. Ben and I followed him. I had this horrible sick feeling in my stomach, and my legs and arms felt like they were made out of rags and stuffing. Nobody spoke a word the whole drive over to wherever it was that Mr. Purvis was heading.

Finally we reached this place on the other side of town. It was an old house that had once been a beautiful plantation home but that had been left to rot. It had six big columns out front and a rusting metal roof. You had to drive up a long driveway lined with oak trees to reach it. When we got there we saw three Yallee County Sheriff's department cars pulled up in the weedy yard, their lights throwing blue flashes up on the peeling white walls of the house. Then I saw a fourth car behind them. It was Mom's Volvo.

"Chass, you better stay in the car," Mr. Purvis said as

we pulled up to the house. But when he got out of the car, Ben and I climbed out, too.

"Mom!" I called.

Despite the sheriff's department cars, there was nobody outside the house. We hurried up the sagging steps and into the house. I could hear something going on down in the basement, a hollow, eerie clanging that reverberated through the whole house, making the floors and walls shake. Oddly, the house was full—not just with old mildewed furniture, but with all kinds of random junk, crumbling cardboard boxes stacked up three and four high, old newspapers in piles, empty liquor bottles, old clothes. It looked like somebody had just walked out of the house twenty or thirty years ago, leaving everything they owned behind.

"Sheriff?" Mr. Purvis called. "Anybody?"

"Mom!" I yelled. "Mom!"

The eerie clanging stopped, and then somebody came clumping up the stairs. A man came around the corner, a man I recognized as Sheriff Doyle Arnett.

The sheriff stopped when he saw Ben's dad, and his eyes narrowed. "Purvis," he said, his voice vaguely contemptuous. "What in the samhill are you doing here?"

"I got a call," Mr. Purvis said. He waved one hand in my direction. "This is Allison Pureheart's daughter."

The sheriff's eyes shifted to me, and something in them softened. But only slightly. "I wish you wouldn't of come here, hon," he said.

"Where's my mom?" I said.

"Let's talk outside," the sheriff said.

Whatever southern sheriffs were supposed to be like—big tough dudes with dark sunglasses and double chins—he was pretty much the opposite. Sheriff Doyle Arnett was small and delicate featured, with hands that looked kind of oily, like he had spent most of the afternoon squeezing lotion on them. He didn't even have a sheriff's uniform but instead wore a charcoal gray suit that looked like it had cost a whole lot of money, and a striped shirt with the kind of cuffs that get folded back and have those little gold ringy-ding things instead of buttons. His hair was blond and glittered from all the hairspray he'd put in it. The only way you'd even know he was the sheriff was this tiny silver star, smaller than my thumbnail, that he wore pinned to his lapel.

He turned and walked out the front door. We followed him out onto the veranda. "Watch where you step," he said. "One of my boys already put a foot through the boards." He pointed at a jagged hole in the rotted flooring. When we had gotten down to the yard, he put one hand softly on my arm. I could feel my heart beating, and

I could barely stand up. For some reason I didn't really want this man touching my arm.

"Chastity," he said, "your mama's not here."

I could hear the banging noise start back up inside the house. "Where is she?"

The sheriff shook his head. "I don't know, hon."

I pointed to her car, feeling wave after wave of desperation wash over me. "But . . . that's her car!"

"We know that," the sheriff said.

"Then what . . ." I tried to think of something else to say, but I couldn't make any more words come out.

The sheriff turned to Mr. Purvis—and again a look of naked contempt came into his eyes. "Purvis, you and your boy go set in your car. I need to have a little talk with the young lady."

"I'd prefer to be there with her."

Sheriff Arnett gave him a long look. "Go set in the car."

Mr. Purvis looked back at him. I got the sense there was some kind of conflict between the two men that went back a long, long way. Finally Mr. Purvis turned to Ben and said, "Come on, son."

The sheriff waited until they were in the car, then he turned to me. Before he had a chance to speak, a deputy came out the front door and said, "We busted it down like you said, Sheriff."

"And?"

The deputy shook his head. "Nothing."

"Then y'all get busy securing the crime scene," the sheriff said.

Crime scene. Just the sound of those words made me feel nauseated. "What is going *on* here?" I said.

The sheriff mashed his lips together, then he blew a bunch of air out of his mouth, letting his cheeks puff up like a chipmunk's. This was obviously supposed to make me think he was the most sympathetic guy in the world, that he really cared about me and all my problems. Which I suspected he did not. "Earlier this morning a couple of idiots cut school and came down here to smoke stuff they shouldn't be smoking. They snuck in the back door. Inside the house they found . . . ah . . ." He cleared his throat. "They found a certain quantity of what looked like blood. And a purse. They came back outside, noticed your mama's car. I guess word's got around town that your mama went missing, so they called 911."

"Who was it?"

"Ricky Spence. Joey Chisman."

He was right. They *were* idiots. They were in my grade, a couple of dopers who always went around giggling at stuff that nobody else seemed to find funny.

"But Mom's not here?"

"No. We've taken some blood samples. We'll send

them up to the crime lab. We'll need to get a hair off your mom's hairbrush or something, see if we can't come up with a DNA sample, find out whose blood that is in the house."

Suddenly I had to sit down. I went over to the steps and collapsed on the rotting wood. Sheriff Arnett came over and sat next to me. Again he put his hand on my arm. And again I didn't like it.

"This doesn't mean anything," he said. "Not yet."

"Mom wouldn't leave me by choice," I said. "She wouldn't leave her car either."

"Down in the basement there was a sort of . . ." He broke off and said, "Look, your mama's not here. Let's not jump to conclusions, all right?"

"How much blood?" I said. "What's in the basement? What happened in there?"

"You don't want to be thinking about that."

My tone got a little sharper. "What was in that basement?"

But the sheriff didn't say anything. He seemed to be considering something, like he was making a decision about how he wanted to go about talking to me. Finally he took some things out of the pocket of his suit coat and set them on my leg.

"Take a look at those," he said to me.

I picked up the stuff he'd put in my lap. It was six

separate plastic Baggies with red letters on them that said EVIDENCE. DO NOT OPEN. I didn't have to open them to see what was inside. Each one held a plastic ID card. One was a Kentucky driver's license for somebody named Ellen Carter. One was an ID for a woman named Gillian Oberdorf. Another was an ATM card from a bank, the kind with a photograph on the front. Another was a company ID card. All the names were different. But the face in the picture on each card was identical. It was my mother.

"Where did you find these?"

"Your mama's purse and cell phone were in the basement." Sheriff Arnett paused. When he spoke again, his voice had taken on an insistent note. "What do you know about these IDs, young lady?"

"Nothing."

And it was true—more or less. Mom had used a lot of different names over the years. But none of these.

The sheriff's eyes narrowed slightly. He had small, pale blue eyes. When he spoke this time, his voice had gone hard. He leaned forward finally and dropped his voice, as though to make sure that anybody who was eavesdropping on us would be unable to hear him.

"Young lady, I take my job real serious. And my job is to make sure that the people in this county keep it between the lines, you get what I'm saying?"

"I'm not sure," I said. Something about the way he was talking made me mad. Like I was some kind of criminal instead of a girl whose mother was missing.

"If we're gonna find out what happened to your mama, we need to know what she was up to."

"*Up to?*" I said.

The sheriff studied my face for a while. "These ain't cheap little ID cards that college girls get off the Internet so they can buy beer, Chastity. These here are top-notch quality. They got holograms, bar codes, the whole nine. I don't believe the CIA could make a better fake ID than these here."

I just sat there staring at the various faces of the woman on the cards. It almost seemed like she was some stranger, a woman I didn't even know.

"Chastity, I don't mean to be running your mama down, but normal, decent-type people don't go around toting fake identification in their purse."

I held the little plastic bags out between my index finger and thumb, then dropped them on the steps between us. "I don't know what you're talking about."

The sheriff had kept a sort of neutral expression on his face for a while, but then suddenly he let it go hard. He leaned toward me. "This here's a good town," he said. "We don't need all kind of vagabonds and criminals coming in here." He squinted at me. "The nut don't fall far from the tree, girlie. I didn't like your mama, not from the minute I slapped eyes on her."

"Is that why you were always hitting on her when she waited on you at the restaurant?" I said.

"My goodness," he said, smiling coolly. "She bites!" Then he leaned back, and the smile faded a little. "Well, look, we're gonna find your mama or we're not. But either way, we need to be taking steps to get you situated."

I didn't have a clue what he was talking about.

"Young lady," he said. "I've just decided to make it my first order of business to get you out of this town. We don't need your trouble here."

"Whatever," I said.

He smiled so I could see all his bright little teeth. "When I get back to my office, I'm gonna lock these ID cards in my desk drawer. I'm not gonna enter them into evidence, I'm not going to type an official investigation report into the computer . . . frankly, I'm not going to do a great deal of anything—not until I get a handle on what I'm dealing with here. Meantime, I'm going to notify the state about your predicament. When they get the paperwork done, the Alabama Department of Human Resources will come down here and drag you away to a foster home where you aren't going to be bothering me or the decent people in this town."

"But I'm staying with Ben!" I said.

"Not if the state of Alabama says you're not." He smiled thinly. "You think about it. Maybe if you start being a little more forthcoming, we can be a little more flexible about your custody situation."

We drove up the dirt road to Ben's house in silence. It was just starting to get dark. Ben's family lives in this old farmhouse outside town. The yard is all bare. There's a big live oak tree out front with a half-rotten tire swing hanging off of it and a bunch of old yard dogs and worn-out appliances lying in the yard, so it looks like they're total rednecks. But they're not. Ben's grandfather used to be some rich muckety-muck that owned half the county or something. But then he blew all the family dough when Ben's dad was a kid. Anyway, Ben's dad went to some famous art school in Rhode Island, and he makes these big goofy steel sculptures that he sells all over the world for not very much money. Ben's mom is kind of a hippie type too. She keeps bees and grows her own vegetables in this huge garden in the backyard. She's really fat and really funny and really nice to me.

We came inside, and Mr. Purvis told Mrs. Purvis about what the sheriff had found at the abandoned plantation house, and Mrs. Purvis cried and gave me this tight hug that went on for a really long time, and just about the time I felt like I was going to scream, the doorbell rang.

Mr. Purvis went to the door and then said, "Sure, I understand, come on in."

A very tall, very black-skinned woman with long, bright yellow fingernails and these kind of fake African clothes came into the room. She was carrying a briefcase in one hand and a cell phone in the other.

"I'm Mrs. Oglesby from the Family Services Division of the Department of Human Resources," she said to me. "You must be Chastity."

"I go by Chass."

"Mmmmmm-hm," she said. She had very heavy eyelids, like she'd had to get the extra-large size to keep the disapproving look in her eyes from exploding out of her head. She ran one of her yellow painted fingernails across the table next to the door, examined the big wad of dust that it had scooped up, and then flicked it away and frowned. Mr. and Mrs. Purvis are not exactly what you'd call great housekeepers. "I'm very sorry about your mother, Chastity," she said. Like the Sheriff, she said it like it was her job to say it, not like it meant anything to her. "Let's sit down."

Mrs. Oglesby lowered herself into the chair real slow and serious, like she was practicing to be queen of some little country in Europe, then she took a notebook computer out of her briefcase and started tapping away at it.

"I'm bringing up your case file, Chastity," she said finally.

"I don't have a case file," I said.

Without looking up, Mrs. Oglesby said, "You do now."

Then she tapped some more and finally looked up. "When a minor's parent deceases prior to that child's maturity, the Family Services Division of the DHR has to step in and establish that a legal and viable custodial arrangement exists for that minor. Your case will then be administratively disposed with all due efficiency. In order to do that, I'll need to obtain certain information. Please consider your answers to my questions and answer them as precisely and succinctly as possible, Chastity."

"My mom's not dead," I said. "And I already told you I go by Chass, not Chastity."

Mrs. Oglesby gave me her disapproving look, letting her eyelids get even heavier and lower. Then after she'd had her fill of staring at me, she looked down at the computer again and said, "Full name."

I could feel my pulse quickening. If she started looking too hard at my background, eventually she'd figure out that I didn't exist. And I didn't want to deal with that. "Chastity Pureheart."

"*Full* name."

"That is my full name."

She gave me the look again, then her long yellow fingernails clicked and clacked on the keys of her computer. "Social?"

"Not really. I'm more of an introvert."

She looked up at me this time like I was stupid. I blinked back at her and pretended like I wasn't jerking her around. "Social *Security* number, Chastity."

"I'd have to look at home," I said. "I don't have the card with me."

She frowned, then stabbed the ENTER key. "Mother's full name?"

"Allison Pureheart. No middle name either." I gave her a fake smile. "It's kind of a family tradition."

"Mother's occupation?"

"Waitress."

"Father's full name."

There was a long pause. "I don't know. I've never met my father."

"Father not known." She said this with a tone of weary superiority, like she heard it all the time. "Date of birth."

I gave her the date.

"Location of birth."

I hesitated. "Uh. Walla Walla, Washington."

"I'll need the names and addresses of your three closest living relatives."

There was a long silence in the room. "I don't have any," I said. "It's just Mom."

For the first time in several minutes, Mrs. Oglesby looked up. "So you have no blood relations who would be available to act as your custodian?"

"Custodian."

"Like a parent," Mrs. Oglesby said. "A legal guardian."

"Why do we have to do this?" I said. "My mother is not dead. She'll come back, I know she will."

Mrs. Oglesby pursed her lips. "The state of Alabama is not in the habit of reading crystal balls. When there is no parent present, certain procedures must be followed. At this time you have no parent."

And I guess that was when it finally hit me that something terrible had surely happened and that I was alone. Completely and totally alone in the world. I started sobbing. Mrs. Purvis came over and put her arm around me, but I kind of pushed her away, and then ran out the back door and sat down on the porch, bawling my head off.

After a while Ben came out and sat next to me. I kind of stopped crying, just sniffling a little, and I could hear the katydids making a racket in the trees, and the sun was all the way down below the horizon, just a small rim of light coming up over the fields behind us. "God, this sucks," I said. "This is so unfair."

Ben cleared his throat. "Mom and Dad and that lady are talking."

"About what?"

He hesitated. "What they're going to do with you."

Somehow my mind hadn't even gotten that far. "Can't I just keep staying with you?" I said.

"That's what they're talking about. Mom and Dad were saying they'd take you in for a while. You know— until things get figured out for you." He hesitated. "But that lady said . . . I don't know, she talks all this mealy-mouth crap, and you never know what she means. She was talking about home studies and adjudication and stuff . . ."

"I better go see," I said.

I went inside to hear how the discussion with the social services woman was going, but as I came into the living room, Mrs. Oglesby was walking out the front door.

Mr. Purvis closed the door and gave me a strained smile.

"This is wrong, Addison!" Mrs. Purvis said to Ben's

dad. Then she saw I'd walked into the room, and her face got all funny.

"What happened?" I said.

Ben's father took a deep breath. "If you want us to, we're going to try to get some sort of custodial arrangement so you can stay with us."

"Whoa!" Ben said. "That's excellent!"

But Ben's parents didn't seem all that happy. "Well. It's not that simple."

"What do you mean?" I said. I had this sick feeling now, like something really bad was going to happen.

"We haven't been approved for foster care. There's red tape involved . . . ," Mr. Purvis said. Then his voice just sort of trailed off.

Ben and I stared at his dad for a minute.

"Look, Chass," he said. "We're going to hire a lawyer and try and get this resolved as quickly as possible. If you want to be here, we want you here."

"Of course I do," I said. "Thank you so much."

Then it was quiet for a minute. Quiet, but not in a good way.

"Tell her," Mrs. Purvis said finally.

"There'll be a temporary, uh, transition period."

"I don't understand," I said.

"*Tell* her, Addison," Mrs. Purvis said.

"You can stay here through Friday night," Ben's dad said. "Then you go into a foster home."

"For how long?"

He shook his head and wouldn't meet my eyes. "I don't know, sweetheart. I don't know."

SIX

BEN'S HOUSE IS real small, and the walls are thin. They don't have a guest bedroom, so I was sleeping on the couch. After I lay down that night, I heard them arguing in their bedroom. They were talking about credit cards and bills and how Mr. Purvis hadn't gotten paid yet for some big sculpture he had made, and how were they going to pay for a lawyer to get custody of me and stuff. It wasn't that they didn't want me there. I could tell they did.

But I also could see that it was going to be a burden

for them. Mr. Purvis was talking about hitting up Mrs. Purvis's parents for a loan, and Mrs. Purvis was talking about going to the bank—and finally I put the pillow over my head. Then I didn't hear them anymore.

Foster home. As sketchy as things with Mom had always been, I'd never been afraid like I was as I lay on that couch with the pillow over my head. Mom always took care of me, was always there for me. Maybe she was a little weird, but she was a great mother. The whole idea of a foster home made me want to throw up. They'd probably stick me with some creepy old child molester who'd chain me to a radiator, and feed me nothing but weevily oatmeal, and take gross videos of me that he'd sell to other creeps on the Internet.

I just couldn't get my mind around the fact that Mom was gone. Was she dead? I refused to believe it. But at the same time, I knew that she wouldn't have taken off by choice. Whatever we'd been running from, it must have finally caught up with us. I lay there crying for a while. Finally I took the pillow off my head. By then the light under the door to Ben's parents' room had gone out, the house was dead quiet, and the moon was throwing some thin light through the window.

Suddenly it hit me. I knew what I had to do. I had the routine down cold by now. How many times had I followed along with Mom as we moved to new places, built our fake identities, started new lives? Over a dozen times by now. I knew the whole drill—how to apply for a Social Security card, where to buy bogus ID cards that you could use to parlay into real driver's licenses and passports and other identification, how to forge birth certificates on a computer. . . .

I knew how to run, and I knew how to take care of myself. Why stick around and let some uncaring jerk from the DHR stick me in a foster home? I could just get my things and leave. All I had to do was grab my bag of clothes and my new guitar, walk down to the highway, and stick my thumb out. I could pass for eighteen if I had to, and I knew enough restaurant lingo from Mom to get a job waiting tables in Atlanta. Nothing to it. Go to a big city and disappear.

I didn't want to leave Ben and his family, and I knew they'd be angry and disappointed. But I just had this bad feeling about foster homes. And besides . . . running was what I did. It was Mom's legacy to me.

I stood, picked up my guitar case and my little backpack full of clothes, and I slipped quietly out the door of the house. It took me a couple minutes to walk the dirt road from the house down to the two-lane highway leading into High Hopes. It was just past midnight.

There were no cars on the road at all. The still, hot, muggy southern air barely stirred. I felt like I'd be frozen there forever, waiting. The katydids in the trees were going *scree scree scree,* and I just stood there with this weird empty feeling inside, like all the juice had been sucked out of me. Suddenly a pair of lights winked on. It seemed odd, not quite like they'd crested the hill coming out of town, but like they just suddenly appeared there a few hundred yards down the road. But it was hard to tell. My eyes were bleary, and I wasn't thinking too straight.

I turned and stuck out my thumb.

The headlights moved toward me, slowed, came to a stop. It was a big Mercedes, new and shiny. The car sat for a moment in the middle of the highway, idling. The moon reflected off the windows, which were tinted dark so that you couldn't see inside. I got the impression that whoever was inside was studying me, making some kind of decision. Like if my boobs were too small or something, he was just going to drive off. He. I was almost sure it was a man inside—though I couldn't say why. I could *feel* him in there.

Then the window hummed, rolled down. I still couldn't see inside the car in the dark.

"Kind of late to be hitching, don't you think?" A man's voice—deep and somehow authoritative. But with a sense of humor too.

"I need a ride," I said.

"Where to?"

"Atlanta," I said.

"I'm not going that far," the man said. "I'm just heading up to Anniston. But you can catch I-20 there, that'll take you to Atlanta."

"Fine," I said.

The door lock clicked, and as I climbed in I wondered what kind of person would have their car locked in an easygoing little hick town like High Hopes, the town where everybody was smilin'.

But by then I was already inside.

My heart was beating a little faster now. The guy didn't look especially pervy or anything, though. He was about thirty, muscular, good-looking, well dressed. Whatever image I had of a perv, he wasn't it. He looked more like a soldier, actually—his hair shaved down so it was barely more than stubble, real straight posture. A guy who looked physically confident.

"I'm Bob," he said. He stuck out his hand, and I shook it. His palm was hard and calloused, like somebody who worked with their hands for a living. Not quite like you'd expect from a guy who drove a Mercedes.

"My name's—" Suddenly I thought: *Now's my chance. I can finally have a name of my own choosing, instead of something that came out of some dumb book.* But I couldn't think of a name that I wanted to say was mine, so I just said, "I'm Chass."

"Cool," Bob said. "You mind if I cut on the radio?"

"I would *love* to listen to some music."

He turned on the radio, and it started playing something classical, a harpsichord. Which seemed odd to me. He didn't look like the classical music type.

"So what brings you out in the middle of the night?" Bob said. "Family trouble?"

"I guess you could say that."

He laughed. "Aren't *we* cryptic."

"I just don't want to talk about it."

He drove a few miles down the little two-lane highway, and then we left the fields behind and got into some woods. The road was totally empty. I don't think we passed a single car. I started humming along with the radio.

Suddenly Bob looked over at me. "You have musical training," he said.

"Huh?" I said.

"Most people, if they knew this piece, they'd hum the melody. It's a Bach two-part invention. You were just humming the counter-melody."

"Was I?"

"You weren't doing it intentionally?"

I shrugged. "I guess not."

"You grow up in a musical family?"

I laughed bitterly. "Not hardly."

He frowned. "Really? That's odd. Music is an extremely heritable trait."

"What's that mean?"

"You know—it's genetic. Like red hair. It runs in families. Who's the musician in your family?"

I didn't say anything.

"Your mother's not a musician?"

I looked at Bob and frowned. He could have said mother *and* father. He could have said *parents*. But he only said *mother*. I wondered why he had said it that way. "Could we talk about something else?"

He raised his eyebrows and shrugged. "Look, Chastity, if you don't want to talk about your family, that's cool. I was just making conversation."

Suddenly I had a bad feeling. It took a minute to figure out why. But then I realized: I'd told him my name was Chass. But he'd just called me Chastity. Which meant he knew who I was before he even picked me up. "You know what?" I said. "Could you pull over? I just realized I really need to pee. Bad."

Bob's face didn't change. He just kept driving.

"Stop, please," I said. "Now."

"You don't want to get out in these woods," Bob said.

"Now!"

"Hey, easy there, tiger." He slowed the car. But instead of pulling over and stopping, he turned onto a gravel track that led off into the woods. Suddenly I knew that this whole thing was wrong. Bad wrong.

I could feel the adrenaline hit me like a brick in the head. I clawed at the door, but for some reason it didn't work, the handle all loose and dead, like it wasn't connected to anything.

"You let me out!" I yelled. "Now!"

He drove about a hundred yards more and stopped the car. We were surrounded by trees and darkness. The branches above me were so thick that the moonlight barely penetrated them. I could see something gleaming in Bob's hand all of a sudden. It took me a second to realize it was a gun. I started shaking.

"This doesn't have to be hard or painful," Bob said quietly.

I just sat there. All I could think was that if I just kept my mouth shut and did what he wanted, it would be over quick and maybe he wouldn't kill me. Why hadn't I stayed at Ben's house? I was a fool to think I could take care of myself. I was only sixteen for christsake. Idiot, idiot, idiot!

"I searched your apartment already," he said.

I tried to open the door again, but with the handle broken, it was a waste of time. I tried to kick Bob in the face, but he blocked my leg and grabbed hold of me like I was just some little kid, not even straining. There was a ghost of a smile on his face. I tried to struggle, but his arm was really strong. Finally I gave up and just lay there.

"Whatever you want," I said finally. "I don't care. Just don't kill me please."

"I didn't find it," Bob said.

I scrunched up my eyebrows and didn't say anything. I didn't understand what he was talking about.

"Very spartan living arrangements, you and your mom's."

I just lay there breathing.

"No books, no records, no stereo, no TV. You both had the exact same number of clothes too. Isn't that odd? Four pants, four short-sleeved shirts, four long-sleeved shirts, one nice blouse, eight bras, eight pairs of underpants. Of course, your mom wore thongs, though, which I thought was fairly adventurous for a thirty-six-year-old mother." He smiled broadly. "But then, she's pretty hot for thirty-six."

"What do you want?" I whispered.

"Just tell us where it is."

"I don't know what you're talking about," I said.

Bob smiled pleasantly, got out of the car, came around to the outside, and opened the door. "My advice, don't scream," he said. "I'd hate to have to shoot you, but . . ." He spread his hands apart like, *Hey, what can I do?*

I got out of the car. It was quiet and dark in the woods, nothing moving at all, no sound but the katydids in the trees.

"There's a shovel in the trunk," he said. "Get it out."

I started running and screaming. "Help me! Help! Somebody!"

I made it about twenty feet before Bob tackled me. Then he turned me over and punched me in the face. It hurt so bad I can't even tell you. God! My whole head ached, and I felt sick to my stomach for a second. Bob sighed loudly. "We feeling a little more compliant? Hm? A little more open to fresh and interesting new experiences?"

I didn't say anything. He let go of me, stood up.

"Go get the shovel," he said, looking down at me.

I got slowly to my feet, walked shakily back to the car. My knees felt like they might give out any second. I could feel blood seeping out of my nose, running down my face. I looked in the trunk. There was a short-handled shovel lying on the gray carpet, the blade slightly rusted. I picked it up and turned around.

"You ever hear on the local news," Bob said, "like, *Girl's body discovered in shallow grave, film at eleven*? You know what I'm talking about?"

I didn't say anything. I could feel my lip quivering. I wanted to cry, but at the same time I didn't want to give this guy the satisfaction. "You've made some kind of mistake here. You're confusing me with somebody else. My name's not even really Chastity."

"That's okay." Bob smiled. "My name's not really Bob either."

I looked off into the woods, hoping to see a light or hear a sound. But there was nothing out there. Nothing for miles and miles.

"See, Chass, I would consider it a personal and professional failure to have to bury you out here," Bob said. "So what I'm going to do is give you an opportunity for thought and self-reflection. While you dig your grave, I'm going to let you think about all the places where it might be. A safe-deposit box, a friend's house, a hole in the backyard. Think about it. Ponder, meditate, muse. When you come up with the correct answer—and I have every confidence you will—you can stop digging your grave and tell me where it is. And I'll let you go."

"I would tell you, I swear to God!" I said. "But I don't know what you're talking about."

"Then you better hope it comes to you." Bob—or

whatever his name was—pointed his gun at the ground in front of my feet. "Start digging, sweetheart."

Have I given the impression that Mom was a crappy parent? I hope not. Because she wasn't.

I admit, she wasn't a normal mother. But she did her best. When your family life is all weird and chopped up like mine is, you don't take parents for granted. Most kids I know are always like, *My mom is such an asshole, she wouldn't let me stay out late on Friday night, and she grounded me, and I hate her, blah blah blah*. And I'd be like, *Huh?* I mean, of course your mom's going to ground you if you're supposed to be in at a certain time and you come back two hours late smelling like you fell in a puddle of vodka. Duh.

I want to stay out late as much as the next girl. But, God, I'd a lot rather have a dad, you know what I mean? I never had the luxury of taking my parents for granted.

When you're like me, you tend to study other kids' parents, other kids' families. And for all the weirdness of my life, and for all the strange stuff Mom's dragged me through, the one thing I'd say about her is that she never made me feel small. A lot of kids' parents make their kids feel like morons all the time.

Not Mom.

I don't mean she didn't have rules or she didn't punish me when I got out of line. But Mom always made me feel like her partner in crime. Was it just because she was lonely? I don't know. Mom was cool.

No, she *is* cool. I'm not going to talk about her in the past tense anymore.

When I was a very little girl, I didn't know that most people didn't live like me and Mom. I didn't know that you didn't just pick up and move on half an hour's notice.

See, Mom was good about it. When the time came to run, she didn't act all panicky. She didn't try to scare me. Maybe she was a little stiff, a little nervous. But still, she was very matter-of-fact. We always had everything ready to go. Always. Suitcases by the door. Toothbrushes packed. *Time to go, June Bug*. Then we were in the car and driving.

Mom always made an adventure out of it. She'd play games with me on the way. She'd keep everything light. We'd guess what the next town would be like, what my teacher's name would be, anything to make it seem like jerking yourself out of your old life and heading off for a new one was the most normal thing in the world.

But at a certain point I began to realize that most people didn't live like this. Most people didn't have suitcases with a week's clothing parked permanently by their doors. Most people didn't change their names every year or two. For a while I started to wonder if maybe Mom was just crazy. Thinking—maybe she's paranoid, delusional, schizophrenic, something like that.

But standing there in the middle of those woods with that shovel in my hand and this guy Bob pointing a gun at me? No, I wasn't wondering if Mom was nuts anymore. We'd been running from something real. Real people, bad people. People like Bob.

And I wished more than anything in the world that Mom was there with me. Because Mom would know what to do. *Wouldn't* she?

SEVEN

"START DIGGING," BOB said again.

"What do you want me to dig?"

"A hole," Bob said. "You know, about big enough for a girl your size to lie in."

I put the shovel in the ground and pushed. I knew what he had in mind: I was digging my own grave.

Bob leaned against the trunk of the Mercedes and lit a cigarette while I dug as slowly as I could manage. "You can stop anytime you want," he said after about five minutes. He grinned. "I mean, provided you tell me where it is."

"I don't know what you're talking about!"

"Safe-deposit box? One of those self-storage places? She bury it in the backyard, maybe?"

I didn't answer, just kept digging.

"Anytime," he said. "Tell me where it is, you can stop digging, I'll hop in the car and drive away."

"If I knew what you were talking about, dude, I swear to God I'd tell you," I said. "But I have no idea."

Bob dropped his cigarette on the ground, stubbed it out with the toe of his shoe. "That's a shame. I hate the idea of killing you. I mean, I've killed females before. But nobody as cute as you. Or as young. It would weigh on my conscience." He laughed. "For about three minutes anyway."

"I don't *know*!" I said.

"Maybe you know where it is, but you don't know that you know. See what I mean?"

"No."

"For instance, you ever go to the bank with your mom and she gets a safe-deposit box and puts something in it that she doesn't show you? A locker at a bus station? Or a friend that you go to visit every year at a particular time? A lawyer maybe? An accountant?"

I wracked my brain, but I couldn't think of anything.

"Keep thinking while you dig," he said.

I dug some more, and then I saw headlights through the woods coming toward us. In the blackness I couldn't make out anything about the vehicle.

"Was somebody following you?" Bob said.

"Of course not."

Bob frowned at the lights.

As the headlights wound closer, Bob concealed the gun behind his back. "All right, Chastity. Whoever it is, just be cool. You're a biology student at the University of Alabama, and I'm with the, ah, state agricultural extension service. We're out collecting . . . botanical samples. Okay? Some kind of rare fungus that glows in the dark or whatever. That's why we're here at night. Got it?"

I didn't say anything.

"Now, sweetheart, if you scream or in any way call attention to our little situation here, I'll kill you *and* whoever's in that car. Clear?"

I nodded.

The headlights were getting closer and closer. Suddenly I heard the car gun its engine and head straight toward us.

I couldn't believe it. It was the Batmobile! Ben? How did he find us? The Batmobile was tearing down the bumpy clay track, heading straight toward the Mercedes.

Bob looked quizzically at the oncoming lights. From

where he was standing he couldn't watch me and the headlights at the same time. I started waving my arms. Ben accelerated toward us. Bob looked at me, saw me waving, then pulled his gun out from behind his back, aimed it at the car. Bob must have realized at that point that Ben wasn't going to swerve because instead of shooting, he got a panicky look on his face, and tried to jump out of the way. But it was too late. There was a huge metallic bang and the Batmobile smashed into the Mercedes, crushing Bob's legs and hips between the two cars.

Bob's eyes got wide and went, "You hit me! You son of a bitch, you hit me!" He stared down at the wreckage of his body like he couldn't believe what he was looking at. Then there was blood flowing out all over the place, and his face relaxed, and he folded over like a musician taking a bow and didn't move anymore.

Ben jumped out of the Batmobile and looked at Bob. "Oh man!" Ben said. "Oh *shit*!"

"How did you get here?" I said.

Ben just kept looking at Bob, lying there with his cheek against the crumpled hood of the car. Blood was coming out his mouth and his nose now.

"Oh man," Ben kept saying. "I think I killed him."

"Let's go!" I shouted.

"But what about—"

"Let's *go*!"

I jumped into the Batmobile.

"I think he's dead," Ben said.

Suddenly Bob twitched. He seemed to be trying to push himself up with one arm. He still had the gun clutched in his hand.

"Now, Ben!"

As soon as Ben saw the gun, he hopped back in the front seat of the Batmobile, gunned the engine, threw it in reverse. I could hear rocks and dirt flying up from the back tires, pinging on the floor of the car. One of the headlamps had gone out, and the other had been knocked cockeyed. But it was enough for us to see Bob's body fall in a heap, his legs collapsing under him like bags of sticks.

Ben cut the wheel, and we tore down the bumpy road so fast that my head banged off the roof.

We hit the highway, and Ben cut the wheel hard. The tires howled.

"Oh my god," Ben said. "Oh my god. Oh my god. Oh my god."

"Dude, you are my total hero," I said. I put my arms around him and kissed him on the side of his face. "How did you find me?"

"I heard you leaving." He hesitated. "So I kind of watched you out the window. And when that car rolled up, I don't know, I just got nervous. I mean why's some guy with blacked-out windows driving around picking up girls at one o'clock in the morning? It didn't seem right. So I just followed you."

The car was silent for a while, nothing but the thrum of the big old engine.

"What are we gonna do?" Ben whispered finally. "I think I hurt that guy pretty bad. What are we gonna do?"

"We're going to go back to your house," I said, "and we're going to get in bed."

"And then what?"

"I don't know," I said. "I'm thinking."

But the fact is, I didn't have any ideas.

Have you ever known somebody—or thought you knew them—and then something happened, and suddenly it was like, whoa, this person is totally different from who I thought they were? And it's like you're looking at them for the first time? When I met Ben he was this skinny, geeky kid with not-so-great skin. That's who I had in my mind when I looked at him every day.

But now I was sitting there with my arms halfway around him, and I realized I hadn't really looked at him— really *looked* at him—in ages and ages and ages. His face was a whole different shape than how I had him in my mind. Squarer. More, uh, manly. I know that sounds really gay and everything, but that's how it was. I had this skinny, pimply fourteen-year-old kid in my mind, but the guy sitting here—well, he was still kind of skinny, but he was definitely a man now. He was more rangy than skinny. And his skin was fine, and his eyes were this deep intense black. His hair was a mess, but kind of in a cool way. His clothes were crappy—but, like I say, kind of in a cool way.

I felt this weird sort of sizzle in the middle of my chest, like *ksshhhhh*, looking at him. But then I just rammed it back down and made it go away. He was my best friend. You couldn't get all goony about your best friend. It would ruin everything.

But all the way back to his house I kept feeling his face on my lips.

Kssshhhhhh.

EIGHT

AFTER WE GOT back to Ben's house, I lay there in the dark on the couch in Ben's living room, staring at the ceiling and thinking about my life. What was it all about? Why was it that this guy Bob, a guy I'd never seen before, never talked to—how come he seemed to know more about my life than I did? I mean there was something crucial, something central to who I was that he knew . . . and I didn't.

Don't I have a name? I kept thinking. *Don't I have a story? Don't I have something?*

I had to find Mom. Mom would have the answers. I knew she would.

The next morning I got up, walked out to the road, and picked up the paper, the *Yallee County Advocate*. It was lying on the grass in a plastic wrapper, lightly covered with dew.

A long time ago, Mom had told me that there was a distant possibility that she and I might get temporarily separated. If it happened, she said, she would leave a classified ad in the local paper of whatever town we were in that would tell me where we could meet.

The ad would be in the real-estate section. It would look like this:

ROOM FOR RENT. CHILDREN, YES. PETS, YES. SMOKERS, NO. LOUD MUSIC, NO. 104 SQUARE FEET. CALL MRS. CHURCH ON WEDNESDAYS ANYTIME AFTER 6 PM.

What that meant was that she was going to meet me at 104 Church Street on Wednesday at six o'clock in the afternoon. If it had said 1212 square feet and Mrs. Third, then we would meet at 1212 Third Street. And so on.

I opened the paper, flipped to the classified ads. I don't

know if I was really expecting something to be there. But I was sure hoping.

My heart was beating fast as I thumbed through the paper, scanned through the real estate ads. As I read, my heart began to sink. I read through the ads three times. But there was nothing there.

I went inside and gave the paper to Mr. Purvis. Ben's father said, "Oh, that's really sweet of you, getting the paper for me."

"Sure," I said.

Ben came out a few minutes later, took a shower, brushed his teeth. Then we drove to school in the Batmobile like nothing had happened the previous night. Like life was normal.

All day at school people were looking at me funny. I knew what they were thinking: *Did you hear about Chass? About her mother? Isn't that sad and weird and pathetic?*

But nobody said anything to me. Nobody except Brittany Arnett. Brittany is the sheriff's daughter. She's the bitchiest girl in the whole school, but she's also the most popular, the most beautiful, all that stuff. She never talks to me. But today she stopped in the middle of the hall and went, "God, Chass, are you okay?"

"Huh?" I said. Having Brittany Arnett recognize my presence was totally unexpected; usually if she noticed me at all, it was to make some snotty remark about my clothes or something.

"Daddy told me about your mom," she said. "God, that is so terrible!" She had her eyes real wide open and the tips of her upper teeth showing, which is the face all the cheerleaders make when they're trying to look sympathetic.

"Yeah, well," I said.

"Can I do anything?"

I shrugged. "Thanks," I said. "But no."

Then she gave me this big hug and walked off. Weird. I halfway thought maybe she was making fun of me.

Last class of the day. Mr. Sherman, history. *The* most boring teacher on the planet. He wears the same brown polyester necktie every day and lives with his mother.

Mr. Sherman started telling us how we had to write a paper for High Hopes History Day, something about an event that had happened in the history of High Hopes, Alabama. All day my mind had been going around and around and around about my mom, and about the guy Bob who wanted to kill me, and about my lips on the side of Ben's face, and all this stuff. Everybody was shooting spitballs and hiding Game Boys under their desks and stuff, and suddenly it hit me.

"You mean like if I wanted to find out the history of

a particular house or something?" I said, raising my hand. "Like who lived there? And if something had happened to the house, why? Like if it was abandoned or something?"

Mr. Sherman put his hands together like he was praying and squinted at me. "May I say," he said, "that I'm sincerely heartened to see that someone has put their thinking cap on. That's a charming idea, Chastity. Did we have a particular home in mind?"

"Maybe," I said.

"If you're looking for information on a subject that narrow, let me commend you to speak with Ms. Pennybreaker over on Sugar Mill Road. She's something of the unofficial historian of our fair city." A spit wad hit Mr. Sherman in the neck, but he just droned on, not seeming to notice.

Ben had to go straight to work from sixth period, so I was going to have to ride the bus back to his house. I was walking out to the bus ramp when a bright green car rolled up next to me. It was Brittany Arnett. "He-eyyy!" she called to me. "Need a ride?"

I got in the car. "What is this, charity-for-geeks week down at First Baptist?" I said.

She looked at me like, *huh*?

"Come on. You normally wouldn't even talk to me, much less give me a ride," I said.

Brittany took out her lip liner, repositioned her lips.

68

"Honey," she said, "you can get out if you want. I was just trying to be nice."

"Okay. If you say so."

As I settled into the seat, she peeled out, pelting a couple of nearby freshman with gravel. Her car was brand-new, a Mustang convertible with a big growly engine. She pulled out a pack of cigarettes, shook one out. "Mm?" she said, holding the pack out to me.

"Nah."

"I would have thought you'd be a smoker," she said. "Playing guitar and wearing all those freak clothes and everything."

"I would have thought you'd be at cheerleading practice."

She made a dismissive farting noise with her lips. "*Cheer*leading," she said sarcastically, firing up her cigarette. "So. This report for Mr. Sherman. You're gonna write about that house, aren't you. Where they found your mom's car?"

"Maybe."

"I could take you to see that old lady if you want." She opened the sunroof, blew smoke up toward it. "She's totally nuts, but she does know a lot about the town."

"Why are you interested in this?" I said. "Why do you suddenly care about my life?"

Brittany's face got hard. "I told you I'm—"

"I know, you're being nice. But seriously. You don't expect me to believe that, do you?"

For a second she looked like she was going to jam on her brakes and push me out of the car. But then suddenly she grinned. "You're not as dumb as you look, you know."

I was about ready to strangle her. "Hey, Brittany, I can just walk."

"Come on, come on." She batted her eyes at me and showed me all the nice work her orthodontist had done on her teeth. "I'm just *joking*. God!"

We drove for a while past a lot of soybean fields. Our high school is way out in the country for some reason, instead of in the middle of town. I sort of studied her out of the corner of my eye. Your first impression of her was perfect hair, perfect teeth, perfect boobs, perfect everything. But the more I looked at her, the more I could see how hard she'd worked to put it together. Actually her nose was a little crooked, and under all that makeup her skin wasn't so fabulous, and she might even have been wearing a padded bra. I don't know why, but for a moment I felt a little sorry for her. All that effort— she must be practically paralyzed with fear that for half a second somebody might think she wasn't entirely flawless.

"Go ahead, spit it out," I said. "I can see you're dying to say something."

"You ever watch any of those shows on TV?" she said finally. "Like *CSI*? Or *Law and Order*? Man, I love that stuff."

"Ah," I said. "You're sucking up to me all of a sudden because you want to be Nancy Drew?"

She made a sour face. "All these girls around here are so *dumb*. I hate them."

"Then why do you hang out with them?"

She shrugged, still staring sourly out the window. Then her face brightened. "But come on, Chass! Wouldn't it be cool? We could figure out what happened! I could help you. My dad's the sheriff, you know. I could find out everything he knows and then we could—"

"Hey!" I said, poking my finger in her face. "This is my life. This is not some damn TV show. Okay?"

She flushed. "Yeah. Yeah, okay."

"Why do I even need your help?"

Brittany slammed on the brakes, pulled over to the curb. "You don't have any friends here, Chass. Nobody knows you. Nobody likes you. This is a little close-knit town that's suspicious of people like you. You know what they say behind your back? All kinds of stuff. Whatever happened to your mom, if it's got anything to do with people around here, well, sweetie, you can forget about anybody helping you." She glared at me for a while. Then suddenly she gave me that smile again, with the wide eyes and the tips of her perfect teeth showing. "Unless . . . somebody like me is helping you."

"Ben will help me. He's from around here."

She laughed. "Yeah. Ben. Like *that* freak would be any use to you."

"He's not a freak."

Brittany threw her cigarette out the window. "This is that old lady's house that Mr. Sherman told you about. Let's go."

For a minute I thought about telling her to go to hell. But then I thought, *you know, maybe she's right.* Maybe she *could* help me.

Ms. Pennybreaker was a tall, mannish woman. I want to say she was like ninety years old, but maybe she was just prone to wrinkles, I don't know. Her hands shook constantly, and she leaned on a cane that had all kinds of weird little designs that I couldn't quite make out carved into it. Her house must have been about a thousand years old, and nothing in it looked like it had been made any later than the Civil War. There were old, old black-and-white photos on the wall—bearded men in uniform and women in dark dresses with slightly crazed expressions on their faces.

"So," Ms. Pennybreaker said finally, "Mr. Sherman sends me a handful of students every year, and most of them turn out to be the worst kind of fools." She had a bright, cheerful expression on her face. "Some reason I should think you're different?"

"Well, ma'am," Brittany said, her hands carefully folded in her lap, "we're *extremely* interested in history. And we're both straight-A students."

"Straight-A students!" The old lady cackled and raised one eyebrow. She looked at me. "Is this girl for real?"

"Not really," I said.

Ms. Pennybreaker took out a pack of Marlboros. "You girls want a smoke?"

"No, ma'am," Brittany said, still looking like she was auditioning for the church choir. "We don't smoke."

"Just 'cause I'm old doesn't mean I have a pole up my rear end or a bowl of grits for a brain. I saw you throwing your cigarette out the window when you pulled up in that overpowered little car of yours."

Brittany said, "Uh . . ."

"That's what I thought," Ms. Pennybreaker said. She rearranged her cane against the arm of the chair. Now that I was closer, I could see that the carvings on her cane showed people being eaten by monsters with bulging eyes and tongues hanging out of their mouths. It didn't look like something a normal old lady would carry. "Now what do you girls want to know about?"

"The abandoned house on Folger Street," I said. "I want to write a history of it for High Hopes History Week."

"Well *now*!" she said. "Maybe y'all aren't as dumb as you look." She narrowed her eyes for a minute, looking at me. "What did you say your name was again?"

"Chass Pureheart."

Suddenly her face softened. "Ah. I see. It's your mother, the one who disappeared there."

I nodded.

She fired up her cigarette with a kitchen match that she flicked against the thick yellowed nail of her thumb. She took a long, thoughtful drag on it. "And what's your angle?" She pointed her Marlboro at Brittany.

Brittany said, "I just thought I could help. Being that I grew up around here and Chass didn't, I figured maybe I might know some people who she wouldn't."

"Y'all two girls don't seem chummy, is why I ask." She looked back and forth between us. "Don't dress the same, don't act the same—you don't look much like you even like each other. Did Mr. Sherman assign you to do this together?"

"No, ma'am," Brittany said.

"So you're helping Chass here out of the goodness of your heart."

Brittany wrinkled her nose but didn't answer.

"Honey," the old woman said, "how about you go sit out in your shiny little car while Chass and I talk."

"But—"

"Bye-bye." Ms. Pennybreaker smiled maliciously and waved a crooked old hand. "I'd see you to the door, but my arthritis has got me all tied up in knots right now."

Brittany left in a mild huff.

Ms. Pennybreaker waited until she was gone then said, "Poor old Sheriff Arnett has just spoiled that little girl rotten. His wife has trouble with her plumbing, and Brittany was the only child they could have. Everything she ever wanted, she's gotten. I don't trust her a lick."

I didn't say anything.

"Do you trust her, Chass?"

"I don't even really know her."

"Then why . . ."

"She just picked me up after school and said, 'Let's go see Ms. Pennybreaker.'"

Ms. Pennybreaker looked thoughtful, then stubbed out her cigarette. "So. What is it you want to know about the old Purvis place?"

I must have blinked and looked kind of stupid for a minute. Purvis—that was Ben's last name. "Purvis?"

The old woman smiled a little. "So you really don't know *anything* do you?"

"Is that the same Purvis as Addison Purvis?" Addison was Ben's father's name.

"Sure. Addison grew up in that house."

"What happened? How come he doesn't own it anymore?"

Ms. Pennybreaker pulled out another cigarette, put it behind her ear, then set the pack of Marlboros on the table. "You want the long story or the short story?"

"Long, I guess."

"Here's the problem. I don't know the long story."

"Well, who does?"

"Nobody!" The old lady gave me a mischievous smile. I had the feeling she was messing with me. Or testing me. I couldn't tell which.

"What am I missing?" I said.

"What you're missing is, I'm not spoon-feeding you the story. If I did, you'd miss something important. Plus, it would mean you wouldn't have to do any work. What I can do is point you in the direction you need to go. I'll give you the short story, then it's up to you."

"Okay."

"The short story is, Addison's daddy had inherited several very large farms, a great deal of rental property, and a lot of acreage in this county. By the time Addison was born, his daddy hadn't exactly squandered his inheritance, but he hadn't much worked his fingers to the bone keeping it either. He and Addison's mama were always flying off to France and such. But then when Addison was about ten years old, his mama passed away. I guess she'd kind of kept Addison's daddy—his name was Hughes, Hughes Purvis III—she had kind of kept Hughes in check. But after she died, Hughes went off the deep end. Drinking, running around, playing cards, flying to Las Vegas and New York, and so on—and pretty soon he was selling off all his property to pay for his crazy lifestyle. Then one day something happened in that house. Or maybe it didn't."

"What do you mean?"

"It was when Addison was about seventeen—whatever it was. Or wasn't. Addison left town pretty soon after that. We didn't see Addison for another ten years. After his daddy died, Addison came back. He had long hair, big old beard, funny clothes. Said he'd become a *sculptor!* People around here, they'd never even *seen* a sculptor. Anyway, far as I know, he still owned his daddy's place, but instead of moving in there, he took over a little farm his daddy had owned, and he left the old house to rot. Far as I know, the county took it back for nonpayment of taxes. But I could be wrong."

The house was silent for a while. The lights were dim, and the shutters were closed on the windows, and big slants of light cut through the dusty air.

"You know, Ms. Pennybreaker," I said, "what I'm really trying to find out is what happened to my mom. Honestly, I don't really care about this history report."

"I know that, sweetheart," the old woman said. "But either your mama was there for a reason or she wasn't."

Suddenly I was crying. "I don't know why I thought I was going to get any answers out of that old house. I miss my mom so much."

The old lady came over and cradled my head in her arms. "Don't give up yet," she said.

I stopped crying after a while.

"Have you ever heard of Jimmy Laws?" she said finally.

"The singer?" Jimmy Laws was a semifamous singer who had lived in High Hopes when he was a kid. He had died back in the '80s, and everybody in High Hopes always talked about him like he was some huge deal—though I didn't really know who he was until I moved there.

"You want to know more about that house? Look into Jimmy Laws."

"But . . . how?"

Ms. Pennybreaker walked slowly over to the door, leaning on her strange, carved cane. "Go. Nothing else I can do for you. Time's a wastin', as they say."

NINE

WHEN I GOT back to Ben's place, Ben's dad was working in his barnlike work shed behind the house, standing on a ladder, welding a giant hunk of steel. Sparks flew through the air. I got myself a glass of milk and then walked out to the shed. "I'm home," I called to him.

It felt strange saying that. This was not *my* home.

Ben's dad flipped up his welder's mask so I could see his face. "How you holding up?" he said.

I shrugged. "Fine, I guess." I didn't feel fine.

Mr. Purvis looked down at me from the ladder. "Where's Ben?"

"Work."

"Oh, I forgot." He smiled wanly. "Well. Make yourself at home."

"Yeah," I said. He reached up to flip his mask back down, but then I said, "So. That place where they found Mom's car . . ."

He looked at me expressionlessly.

"You didn't tell me it was where you grew up."

Mr. Purvis looked off into the distance. "I don't have lots of happy memories about that house," he said finally.

"What do you think they were doing in the basement?" I said. "What was all that banging?"

He shook his head vaguely, gave me a silly, blank look.

"I mean, was there evidence down there? Did the sheriff have reason to think she'd been down there?"

Ben's father cleared his throat. I got the sense he was hiding something from me. "Look, if the sheriff had news about your mother, he'd tell you."

"You and him didn't seem to get along too great," I said.

"We don't," he said. He was suddenly starting to look irritated at all my questions.

"The reason I'm asking about the house," I said, "is I have to do a history report for Mr. Sherman's history class and I thought I'd do it about that house."

Mr. Purvis's face got hard. He jabbed the point of his welder toward me. "That house is falling apart. It's very dangerous. I don't want you and Ben getting clever ideas about going inside there."

I hadn't said anything about going in the house. In fact, it hadn't even occurred to me until that moment.

"I'm dead serious, Chass. You and Ben are absolutely not to go in that house. Are you clear on that?"

"Okay."

Mr. Purvis put a sickly little smile on his face. "So, look, I'd love to chat, but I'm running up on a deadline with this sculpture. It's supposed to be in Portland by next week, and I don't even have all the fabrication done yet." He flipped down the mask and started sending a shower of angry sparks down from the steel.

I turned and walked back to the house with an uneasy feeling. Mr. Purvis was supposed to be on *my* side. Why was he getting all secretive on me?

As I reached the door, I heard the eerie crackle of the welding torch stop. "Chass?"

I turned back toward the shed. Ben's father was looking down at me through the open bay door.

"I forgot to mention," he called to me. "Some guy

phoned you today. Said he was with Iambic Records. Does that mean anything to you?"

I shook my head.

"Number's by the phone. His name's Justin or Jason or something."

"Thanks."

I went back inside and found the note.

JUSTIN TAYLOR—IAMBIC RECORDS— URGENT.

The number was for the 213 area code. 213. I'd lived in the 213 area code before. That was Los Angeles. My palms started sweating. Could it have something to do with Mom's disappearance? Maybe Mom was having somebody call me on her behalf.

I still had Mom's cell phone. She could call long-distance for no charge. I turned on the phone, called the number. My hands were shaking.

"Justin Taylor!" The voice was upbeat, obviously a grown-up, but with a youthful edge.

"Hi," I said. "Uh, my name is Chass Pureheart. I got a message you called."

"Chastity! Hey! Excellent! Love that name, dude. That's your stage name, right? I mean, that can't be your real name, huh?"

Kind of ironic that that was his first question. "Uh. Yeah," I said. "It's my real name."

"No kidding! Well, hey, I bet you're wondering why I'm calling."

"If you're trying to sell me some record club membership or something . . ."

Justin Taylor laughed loudly. "Nah, nah, dude. I'm in A&R for Iambic Records."

A&R. I had read enough about the music business to know what that meant. A&R people were the guys who signed new acts for record companies. "Okay . . . ," I said.

"Reason I'm calling, I just had a copy of this demo of yours come across my desk."

"Demo," I said. I was really coming across like an idiot. But I couldn't figure out what this guy was talking to me for.

"Yeah, it's got two songs on it. 'This Is the Real Me' and 'Twilight'?"

Suddenly I knew what he was talking about. Ben had this friend named Doug Slayton who worked at a record store and had a little studio in his back bedroom. A few months earlier I had gone over to Doug's house, and he'd recorded me singing two of my songs. Doug had burned me a couple of CDs when we were done. Then he'd said he was going to make some more and send them out as demos to a few record labels. A demo was a recording you sent to a record company when you were trying to get a recording contract. I figured he was just trying to BS me like he was some big music industry player, and so I'd pretty much forgotten about it. "I just recorded them in one take," I said. "They're kind of rough sounding."

"Yeah, yeah, but the songs, the voice—dude, I'm totally digging them. You wrote the songs?"

"Yeah."

"They weren't cowrites?"

"What's a cowrite?"

That seemed to stump him for a moment. "You know, like where you write the song with somebody else."

I flushed. "Oh, yeah, yeah, no. I wrote them all by myself."

There was a brief pause.

"You think you could send me a press packet?"

"A press packet." I had no idea what a press packet was. Or why he would want one from me.

"Yeah. Actually a couple of them. And if you've got more songs, a more recent demo, anything like that . . ."

I was feeling way out of my depth. "Can we kind of back up a second?" I said. "What's this all about?"

There was a long pause. "You *are* Chastity Pureheart, right?"

"Uh-huh."

"The singer."

"Uh-huh."

"Okay, so you're a singer, I assume you're looking for a record deal, right?"

"A record deal." The thought of making a record someday had obviously occurred to me. But only in a distant, unreal sort of way. I have a hunch I had a really dumb look on my face. "You want me to make a record for Iambic?"

Justin laughed. "Hold on, hold on, hold on. Let's take it one step at a time. I'd like to start with a press packet. I assume you've got a press packet. You know—photo, bio, a demo, some stuff like that? And maybe a Web site?"

"Yeah, um, see right now I'm kind of revamping all that stuff," I said. "So you kind of caught me at a bad time."

"I assume you're playing out, though, right? Doing some gigs, what, in your area?"

One of the things Mom had taught me to do is that when people started asking personal questions, you took the line of least resistance, agreed with them, made them feel like you were familiar, normal. *Blend in, Chass. Blend in!* Okay, Mom, so I was blending. "Well, yeah, sure," I lied.

"Excellent. Where you playing this weekend?"

"Um." I was so flustered I guess I just sort of wanted

to get off the phone so I could collect myself and process what this man was saying. "Yeah, I'm playing at Ronnie's."

"Where's that at?"

"Uh . . . It's just like this little place here in High Hopes."

Ronnie's was the only bar in High Hopes. I'd been by it plenty of times, watching all the redneck alkies in town slink in and out.

"When you playing?"

"Friday? I think?"

"I got to tell you, dude, there is a lot of interest around the office in this demo. If you've got the goods, I think maybe we'd be very interested in working something out with you."

"Like what? Like a *record* deal?" I said.

"You're playing with me, aren't you," Justin said. "You're being cagey. I like that." He laughed loudly. "Look, I tell you what. I'm flying out to Atlanta this weekend. How far are you from Atlanta?"

"Couple hours maybe?"

"Excellent, what time's your show?"

By this point I was sort of thinking, *Oh hell, this guy's really serious.* But there was no way he'd really come all the way from L.A. to Alabama just to see me. Right?

"Uh. Eight-thirty?" I said.

"Ronnie's, huh? Eight-thirty, Friday? See you then, dude."

The line went dead.

I sat there with the phone in my hand, staring out the back window toward the shed where Ben's dad worked. Sparks were raining down from the sculpture Ben's dad was welding. I felt like running off and burying myself in a hole.

TEN

I CALLED BEN at the restaurant where he worked. "I can't talk," he said. "Mr. Sawyer's been riding me all day."

"Yeah but . . ." I said. Then I told him about the phone call from the record company guy. "I'm just not sure the whole thing's for real," I said finally.

"*Iambic* Records?" Ben said.

"Uh-huh."

"*The* Iambic Records?"

"I guess."

"They're like one of the biggest record labels in the world!"

"I'm in kind of a bind, Ben," I said. "I lied to him. He said he's going to come out from L.A. to see me play. I told him I was playing at Ronnie's. But, I mean, obviously I'm not. I can't even *go into* Ronnie's. Much less play there."

"Whoa!" Ben said.

"I guess I have to call him back and tell him the truth."

"Are you nuts?" Ben said.

"I'll call him back."

I could hear Ben's boss in the background: "Ben! Hey, Ben! Get off that phone!"

"I gotta go," Ben said. "But whatever you do, don't call that dude back. We'll figure this out."

"No, Ben, I—"

"Don't do *anything*, Chass!"

Ben hung up.

I paced around Ben's living room, going crazy with all these thoughts running through my head. It was too much stuff all at once. First my mom, then getting kidnapped, and now this! I decided I needed to do something to keep busy. The old lady Ms. Pennybreaker had said if I wanted to know more about the house, I should find out about

Jimmy Laws. Ben's house was half a mile from downtown High Hopes—not too far to walk—so I walked down to the public library and asked the reference librarian if he knew anything about Jimmy Laws.

It was the same delicate-featured guy who'd been there the day I renamed myself Chastity Pureheart. "Jimmy *Laws*!" he said. "He was a couple classes above me in school. We were all so *crazy* about him."

I just bet you were, I thought.

"We have a whole scrapbook on him as a matter of fact. In our Yallee County history room." He leaned toward me, his eyes widening slightly. "I put it together myself."

The librarian led me into a small room where maps and gloomy old pictures hung on the walls. He hunted around on one of the shelves and finally came out with a three-inch-thick album. He spread it out on the table.

"We've got clippings from his high school days from the *Yallee County Advocate*. That's mostly sports-related and so on. He was a big jock back then. Then of course there's a little bit of a gap after he left town. Then about five years later he started getting famous. I've got articles from *Variety*, *Billboard*, *Spin*, *Rolling Stone*—even one from *People* magazine. Enjoy!"

He scurried away.

I started leafing through the album, looking at the

faded old clippings. Why had Ms. Pennybreaker told me to find out more about this guy? Nothing jumped out at me. The later articles were mostly about his music, the pictures showing him wearing all his cheesy '80s rock-and-roll clothing and his mullet hairdo. Typical music magazine stuff. So I went back to the *Yallee County Advocate* pieces.

LAWS SCORES WINNING TOUCHDOWN. LAWS TAKES PANTHERS TO UPSTATE CHAMPIONSHIPS. JIMMY LAWS DRIVES IN WINNING RUN. LAWS STEALS SHOW IN PERFORMANCE OF *MUSIC MAN*. The pictures showed a cocky blond kid with a snub nose, sucking in his cheeks, trying to look cool. He was cute, I had to admit. With a pretty good build.

The only unusual thing I noticed was that suddenly all the articles stopped in the middle of his senior year. No mention of his playing basketball or baseball that year.

I looked at the last picture in the High Hopes section of the album. It showed three young guys, arms around one another's shoulders, laughing at something that must have been really hilarious. I squinted at the picture. There was something very familiar about the other two boys in the picture. The caption under the photo said: *Three Musketeers. Top Panther scoring threats named to All Up-*

state squad. Quarterback Jimmy Laws (recently signed to a scholarship at University of Alabama), flanked by tight end Addison Purvis, and running back Doyle Arnett. The three longtime pals bring leadership, camaraderie, and excitement to the gridiron. Keep it up, boys!

Longtime pals. Mr. Purvis sure didn't seem like a "longtime pal" of Sheriff Arnett anymore.

I frowned then took the book back out to the reference area and plopped it on the counter in front of the librarian. "Question?" he said.

"Yeah. I'm looking at this, and it's like here he is, Mr. Big-Man-on-Campus, and then suddenly at the end of the football season, he drops off the map for five years. He had a scholarship to University of Alabama. How come there's nothing here about that?"

The librarian pursed his lips. "Well!" he said. "You just cut right to the chase don't you."

"It seems weird is all."

"There were rumors," he said stiffly.

"About what?"

He drummed his fingers on the counter for a moment, then finally said, "Come with me." I followed him to a microfilm machine in another rooom. He took out a piece of microfilm as though he knew the date by heart, scrolled it across the machine. It was old copies of the *Yallee*

County Advocate, a negative image, the words in white, the paper in black. "I know in my heart that he had nothing to do with it. Jimmy just wasn't like that."

Suddenly the images scrolling across the screen stopped. There was a front-page story. *Girl Still Missing After Five Days.*

I read the story. It was about a tenth-grade girl from High Hopes who had disappeared after school one day. They had a picture of her, a brassy-looking girl with a lot of hair. Nancy Rydel was the name under the picture.

"So?" I said.

"She disappeared, and that was that for a while. But then these rumors started going around town that the three musketeers had something to do with it. The Three Musketeers—that's what they called Jimmy and a couple of his friends back then."

"Addison Purvis and Doyle Arnett."

"Right."

"Why did people think they had something to do with it?"

"I think it was just malicious rumors. They were the popular guys, and everybody envied them. But the rumors—they were just *flying* around the town. Somebody was under suspicion of killing Nancy Rydel, somebody was about to get arrested, so on, so forth. And obviously if any one of the three musketeers was going to take the fall, it was going to be Jimmy Laws."

"What do you mean?"

"Oldest story in the book. Addison's and Doyle's fathers were the big cheeses around here. Doyle more or less inherited the sheriff's job from his daddy, and of course Addison's father owned half the county back then. Before he squandered it all. But Jimmy was from the wrong side of the tracks, you might say. So there was nobody to protect him. If somebody was going to go down for Nancy's disappearance, it would be Jimmy."

"So what happened?"

"One day he was just gone."

"That's it? Gone?"

"One day he's at school, the next he's not. It was the day before the state Two-A football championships. The Panthers got stomped into the dirt because he wasn't there. But as soon as he was gone, the whole story about Nancy Rydel—it just died. Nobody knew where he'd gone until he showed up on the radio."

"And Nancy Rydel? Did anybody ever find her?"

He shook his head. "It came out later her father was abusing her little sister and what all. He went to prison for a couple years. Maybe he was doing it to Nancy, too, and she just ran away to get away from him. Maybe he killed her to shut her up." He shrugged. "Who knows."

I thanked him.

"Jimmy's life was such a tragedy. And the way he died? Terrible."

"How *did* he die?" I said.

"It's in there." He pointed at the notebook full of clippings. "Jimmy went out in a boat with some record executive up in New York. The boat sank. He and some other man drowned." The librarian flipped through the album. "Here."

He turned the album around, showed me an article from *The New York Times*. It said that a forty-one-foot yacht had left Southampton, Long Island, early in the evening, run into heavy weather, and capsized. The owner of the boat had survived, while Jimmy Laws and another man died.

I flipped idly through the last few pages of the album.

"That's the last photo ever taken of him," the librarian said wistfully. "He had a concert at Madison Square Garden that night. This was taken backstage."

I looked at the picture. It showed a bunch of jolly-looking young people, all dressed up like 1980-something, the guys wearing mullet hairdos and silk jackets with the sleeves pulled up, the girls in tight leather. Jimmy Laws had his arm around a girl who was laughing, her hair falling across her face. There was something about the picture that piqued my interest—but I couldn't quite place what it was.

I heard a voice behind me.

"Yo, Chass." It was Ben. He was still wearing his stained white dishwashing apron. "Dad said you'd be here."

"I thought you were working," I said.

"I quit," he said, a big smile running across his face. "I never liked that place anyway."

I closed the album. "Why'd you do that?"

"We got important things to do."

"Like what?"

Ben gave me a sphinxlike smile. "Come on, Chass." He snapped his fingers rapidly. "Time's a-wastin'!" He started walking toward the door.

ELEVEN

BEN PULLED THE Batmobile up in front of a single-story brick building with its windows painted black. A couple of seedy-looking old guys were sitting out front on plastic lawn chairs, staring into the late afternoon sun like blind men. The front door was open, but all you could see inside was darkness. A broken neon sign that said COORS LITE dangled in one window.

"What?" I said.

Ben pointed at the crummy-looking building. "Ronnie's."

"I know that."

Ben was grinning at me.

"Oh, come *on*, Ben."

"The guy is flying all the way from L.A. to see you. You can't have him show up here and not have a gig."

"But—"

"But nothing."

I sat there, the windows rolled down in the Batmobile. The two old codgers were staring at us now, unblinking, waiting to see what happened next. *What would my mom do?* I wondered. But I knew the answer. Say what you will about Mom, she was always game for anything. If she were me, she would walk right in there and make something happen. Even if it meant bending the truth. After all, our whole life together had been based on bending the truth, hadn't it?

I jumped out of the car, slammed the door, walked into the bar. It was dim and had a sour smell. I'd never been in a bar before. It looked like some bar from a movie, only crappier. There were booths with tattered black Naugahyde on one side of the room, a couple of scarred-up pool tables in the middle, and a long bar covered with cigarette burns on the other side of the room.

I walked briskly up to the bar. "Hi," I said to the bartender. "Ronnie around?"

"Who?" he said dully. He was a thin, hollow-chested

old guy with buck teeth and a comb-over. He had a toothpick clinging to his lower lip that bobbed when he talked.

"Ronnie?" I said. "Doesn't Ronnie own this place?"

"Ronnie's been dead ten, twelve years. I'm Lon Eddy. I own the place."

I stuck out my hand. The bartender shook it dubiously. "Chass Pureheart," I said. "I'm a singer. I'm looking for a gig."

"We don't got no music here."

I felt a momentary sense of panic, a sense that I should run out the door. But I kept talking. "I'll play for free, though."

"Don't matter. We don't need no music." The bartender looked at me, then his glance went down to my chest. I'm not exactly Miss Chesty. But I'm not flat either. I kept thinking: *What would Mom do? What would Mom do?* I leaned over a little, gave him a better view. That's what Mom would have done. When you're desperate, you do what you have to do.

"Please!" I said. "Pretty please!"

He kept looking at my chest. Finally he said, "Can you sing?"

I nodded enthusiastically.

"Sing something," he said.

I sang "Me and Bobby McGee," the first two verses and the chorus.

"Dadgum, girl! You can flat *sing*," he said. The tooth-pick bobbed up and down on his lip a couple times. "Tell you what, hon—you so hot to play here, slide me fifty bucks, I'll let you put up a tip jar, you'll probably make enough tips to pay me back. How'd that be?"

"Are you serious?" I couldn't believe it would be this easy.

"Okay, okay, okay, twenty-five."

"Yes!" I said. "I'll do it."

The man blinked. "When you say you wanted to play?"

"This Friday. Eight-thirty."

He gave me a cagey look. "I'll need that twenty-five bucks right now."

"Hold on," I said.

I went back outside, leaned into the Batmobile. "Have you got twenty-five bucks?"

"What do you need it for?"

I told him.

"I don't think it's supposed to work like that," Ben said. "He's supposed to pay *you*, isn't he?"

"Oh, come on," I said. "This is your bright idea."

Ben laughed, then he opened his wallet, pulled out the money, handed it to me. I went back inside and laid it on the bar.

He looked at the money, then at me, narrowing his eyes. "How old are you, girl?"

"Uh. Twenty-one," I said.

The toothpick went up and down. He was chewing gum. "Lemme see your driver's license. You look about fifteen years old."

"I don't have my purse on me," I said.

He chewed some more. "All right. But, by golly, I'm checking your ID before you sing on Friday. I ain't gonna have the state liquor board come after me, serving minors in here."

"Hey," I said. "No problem."

I went back outside, sat in the Batmobile, and sighed. "He said he was going to check my ID before he let me play."

Ben gave me a mysterious smile. "Check this out." He pulled something out of his wallet and handed it to me. It was a Georgia state driver's license that said he was twenty-three years old.

"Where'd you get this?"

"Ordered it off the Internet, what do you think?"

"Ben, I have to play in four days," I said. "Even if I ordered it today, it might not get here by Friday."

Ben frowned.

Suddenly something occurred to me. "Fake IDs!" I said.

"That's what we're talking about."

"No, I mean, the sheriff—he had a bunch of fake ID cards that he found in my mom's purse."

"Why would your mom have fake ID cards?"

I had never told Ben about my life with Mom. I had told him that we'd lived in a bunch of places, that Mom liked moving around. But nothing about our identities, our life-on-the-run thing. It had suddenly occurred to me that maybe those ID cards held a clue to her real identity.

"Never mind," I said. "It's nothing."

Maybe I was feeling bold because I'd been able to walk into that bar and fool some old guy into thinking I was an adult. But it suddenly occurred to me that maybe I should get my hands on those ID cards. But how? My heart started thrumming in my chest. There had to be a way.

"So," Ben said. "Friday you're gonna burn that place up. Then that guy from Iambic is gonna make you a rock star. My question is, will you remember us little people?"

I punched him in the arm.

"Ow!" he said.

As we started driving home, I said, "So what do you think happened to that guy? The guy you hit with the car."

The car suddenly seemed very cold, the elation of my lining up a gig disappearing in seconds. "I don't want to think about it," Ben said.

"Maybe we ought to go check it out," I said. "See if he's still there. We should probably call the police if he's just lying there."

"Are you nuts? If he's lying there, he's dead."

"Still . . ."

"No way."

"We have to go look," I said.

Ben sighed and turned onto the highway heading out of town. When the little turnoff into the woods came up, he pulled off and stopped.

"Why do you want to do this, Chass?"

And then I realized. It had nothing to do with calling the police. I wanted to make sure the son of a bitch was dead. "I just do," I whispered. My mouth was dry as a bone.

We turned onto the gravel road, drove slowly down it until we came into the clearing where the man who'd called himself Bob had made me start digging my own grave. The sun was starting to go down, and the light was starting to fade. The big Mercedes sat in the middle of the clearing, its windows dark and impenetrable.

We drove slowly up to the car and stopped. The side of the Mercedes was all dented up. But something was missing.

"Hey, hold on," I said. Ben stopped, and I started to get out.

"Chass, stay in the car."

I got out anyway, walked slowly around the car.

"Oh my God," I said.

"What?" Ben said.

"He's gone. Bob's gone."

The clearing was silent.

"We better get out of here," Ben said.

I ran back to the car, got in, and we started to drive off. "Wait," I said.

"What?"

"We have to go back."

"Why?"

"Just do it!" I said.

Ben put the car in reverse, and we drove back and stopped. I climbed out, leaned into the front door of the Mercedes, opened the glove box. Inside was a white envelope with some papers inside it. I grabbed the envelope then ran back and jumped in the car. "Let's go!"

I couldn't sleep that night. I got up finally and took out my guitar. I didn't want to wake anybody up, so I went out the back door and into Mr. Purvis's studio. It was full of big, heavy, dark machines and chunks of rusting metal. The sculpture he was working on was made of huge, jagged steel plates. It must have been ten or twelve feet high. I didn't like it much. In the darkness it looked like a huge spider, ready to pounce.

I started strumming my guitar, and before I knew it, a song was coming out of me. It was about my mother. I got about halfway through and then ran out of gas.

I knew all these little things about my mother. I knew how devoted she was to me. I knew she loved to eat but never gained any weight. I knew she worked hard at everything she did. I knew she got the heebie-jeebies whenever music came on around her. I knew the color of her eyes, the shade of brown her shoulders turned in the summer, the way she used to murmur to herself when she cooked. I knew how she used to help me with my homework, making it fun and interesting in a way my teachers almost never did, bringing all the ideas alive. I knew that she was educated—too educated to be spending her life waiting tables at one Waffle House after another. I knew the way she'd sometimes stare off into the dark at night when she didn't think you were looking, with this sad expression on her face. I knew she loved me.

But beyond that, what?

I didn't know where she came from or who her parents were or whether she'd been a geek or a freak or a cheerleader in high school. I didn't know where she went to college. I didn't know anything about her *life*. How could you write a song about a person like that? It was like writing a song about a ghost.

Finally I stopped playing and just sat there. After a

minute I heard something behind me. I jumped, wheeled around. There was Ben's dad staring at me. He had tears in his eyes.

"That's an awful sad song," he said.

"You scared me."

"I'm sorry. I heard you get up. Just wanted to make sure you were okay."

I shrugged. "I'm fine."

He came over and sat awkwardly on top of a red metal toolbox next to me. "Chass . . ." he said finally.

I waited.

"Chass, I'm not one to be pessimistic. But I think you need to prepare yourself for the possibility that she's . . ."

"What, dead?"

He nodded silently.

I felt angry at him. My mom was not dead. She was *not*. She couldn't be. I felt like I had to strike back at him.

"Kind of like Nancy Rydel?" I said.

Addison Purvis sat up straight. His face had gone white.

"That house was your dad's house," I said. "Why don't you live in it anymore?"

Mr. Purvis looked at me steadily for a long time. I couldn't tell if he was angry or not. "Man, you're tough aren't you?" he said.

"Seriously," I said. "Something happened there didn't

it? The place is kind of falling apart now, but it must have still been pretty nice when you came back to High Hopes after your father died. You could have moved into that house. Instead you bought this junky little farm way out here. Why?"

"I needed a work space," he said stiffly. "If it's any of your business."

"Jimmy left town about a month after Nancy Rydel disappeared. You waited until the end of the school year to leave. But once you were gone, you didn't come back until your father died. The only person who stuck around was Doyle Arnett. What were you running from?"

Mr. Purvis's jaw was clamped shut. He looked at me but didn't speak.

"My mom went to that house for a reason. And what was all that banging down there? You know something, Mr. Purvis. I know you do."

"I don't know why your mother was there. But I know it didn't have anything to do with . . ."

"Nancy Rydel? The three musketeers?"

"Yeah," he said softly. "With that."

"How do you know?"

He looked off in the distance for a while. "Your mom was not from this town. She didn't know any of us."

"So?"

Mr. Purvis had a funny look on his face. Like he was a little surprised at what was coming out of his own mouth. "I've never spoken to anybody about this before. But there are only two people still alive who know what happened to Nancy Rydel. And it has nothing to do with your mother."

"You and Sheriff Arnett."

"I shouldn't have said anything," he muttered. Not so much to me as to himself.

"You know what happened to—"

He interrupted me. "Sometimes bad things happen. It does no good to anyone to dig them up. Forget about Nancy Rydel. Forget about that house. Whatever happened to your mother, you're going down a blind alley trying to find out about Nancy Rydel."

"Mr. Purvis—"

He stood, pointed his finger at me. "Forget Nancy Rydel. I'm warning you."

"Or else, what?"

Mr. Purvis glared at me for a moment then turned and walked out of the big shed. After a minute the darkness swallowed him up.

I sat there for a while with my guitar on my lap. I used to babysit for this little boy, Frankie Thomas, back when I lived in Ohio. Every time his parents would leave, he'd just sit there for about half an hour rocking back and forth, going, "I want my mommy. I want my mommy." Over and over and over and over.

That's how I felt. Like I wanted to cry and scream like a baby.

Only nothing came out. Nothing at all.

TWELVE

THE NEXT MORNING before school I went out and got the newspaper to see if there was a note in the classifieds from my mother. Again, there wasn't.

As we headed off for school in the Batmobile, I asked Ben if he'd run me by the sheriff's office on the way.

"We're going to be late for first period."

"It won't take two seconds."

Ben looked at his watch, sighed, then steered the car toward downtown.

• • •

Ben parked by the curb. I went inside the sheriff's office and asked a woman sitting behind a couple inches of bulletproof glass if Sheriff Arnett was there. He wasn't. That's what I'd been hoping. I told the woman behind the bulletproof glass that I was supposed to meet him that morning, then asked if I could wait in the sheriff's office.

"Hold on," she said. She talked into a phone for a minute then pointed at a door next to the window. She pressed a button, and the lock buzzed so I could get in.

After a minute a deputy came out and said, "Sheriff Arnett's not in, hon. Something I can help you with?"

"He wanted to talk to me about something. Could I just wait in his office?"

The deputy's eyes narrowed thoughtfully. "How about you wait out in the lobby." He pointed to the other side of the bulletproof glass.

"Okay," I said. I felt a surge of disappointment. "Could I use the bathroom first?"

"I guess so." He pointed down the hallway. "It's right there."

I went into the ladies' room, washed my hands, fiddled around for a minute, then peeked out the door. The deputy was gone. I could see Sheriff Arnett's office at the end of the hallway. I walked briskly down the hallway, into his office, closed the door. My hands were shaking I was so nervous. I couldn't believe I was really doing this. This was the sort of thing Mom might do—but not me. I was always the good girl.

The sheriff said he was going to lock the ID cards in his desk. But where would he have put the key?

I noticed a jar on the credenza. Inside it were some paper clips, a couple of pencils and pens. And a key. A key that was just the right size for the credenza.

Just as I had my fingers on the key, I heard a noise behind me. My fingers closed around the key, then I snatched my hand away, whirled around. Behind me the door had opened. The deputy I'd just talked to was looking at me.

"What in the world are you doing in here, girl?" he snapped.

"I, uh, left my purse in the sheriff's office the other day," I said, holding up my bag and hoping he wouldn't remember I'd had it with me just two minutes earlier. "I guess I should have said. That was the only reason I was here."

"You need to get out of here right this minute."

"Yes, sir," I said.

He grabbed me by the arm and hustled me down the hallway to the door next to the bulletproof glass. "I don't know what you're up to," he said. "But I don't want to see you back here again."

Outside Ben was sitting in the car drumming his fingers. "I hope you got it," he said. "We're already late for first period."

I shook my head glumly. "I almost got caught too."

As I was about to climb into the Batmobile, I saw a green car speeding down the road toward us. I stepped out into the road and waved my hands. The car screeched to a halt and the window went down. Brittany Arnett looked out at me through a pair of very dark sunglasses. "I'm kind of in hurry," she said. "In case you didn't notice."

"Sorry," I said. "But so, look, are you really serious about helping me with my project?"

"Like how?" she said.

I told her what I had in mind.

"You want me to steal evidence out of Daddy's office?" she said. "Are you out of your mind?"

"I know but—"

"Besides, I'm sure it's locked."

I held up the key I had taken from the jar in the office, let it dangle between my thumb and index finger.

She stared at it, eyes wide. "You ripped off his keys? Daddy is gonna freak when I tell him," she said. Then she looked past me, waved her fingertips and batted her eyes at Ben. "Hi, Ben!" she called in a high, flirty voice. Then she snatched the key out of my hand, gunned the engine, fishtailed onto the road, and disappeared in the direction of the high school.

"What's up with *that*?" Ben said when I got back in the car. "Man, Brittany Arnett's never even *looked* at me before. Much less said hello."

I signed. Why had I been stupid enough to trust her? Everybody in the school knew she was a snake. "I think I'm screwed, Ben."

All day I kept waiting for the intercom to click on and hear Mr. Winbush's voice go, "Mrs. Lesley, please send Chastity Pureheart to the principal's office." And everybody would be like "Oooooooo! Chass is in trouble!"

Only it never happened.

What did happen is it seemed like between every class I would see Brittany with all her cheerleader friends, and she'd hold up the key and jingle it, this little tiny smile on her face. Then all the other girls would laugh. The later it got, the more uneasy I felt.

Finally I couldn't stand it, waiting for the guillotine to come down on me. Plus, every minute I spent listening to boring teachers was a minute that I wasn't able to spend trying to find out what had happened to my mother. I felt like I was going to explode. After the bell rang for lunch period, I saw Ben in the hallway waiting in the lunch line. The rank smell of chili dogs was wafting out of the cafeteria. It made me want to throw up.

"Hey, I can't deal with this anymore, Ben," I said. "Can we just bail?"

He looked at me, puzzled. "You mean like, cut school?"

I nodded.

"Chass, you've never cut school in your life. Has an alien taken over your body?"

"All I have is gym and Sherman's class. What's the harm?"

"I've got a test in Mrs. Washington's class," he said.

"Whatever," I said. I turned and walked off.

"Hey!" he called. "Don't be like that!"

I went outside. It was a beautiful spring day, just a few clouds in the sky, perfect temperature. Kids were sitting on the grass, everybody laughing and joking and working on their tans. But it all seemed ominous to me. I went over and sat by myself near the parking lot, pulled something out of my book bag. The white envelope I'd taken from the glove box of the Mercedes.

I opened it and pulled out the papers from inside. One was a vehicle registration from California. It said the Mercedes was registered to an Edward Wong, with an address in Long Beach. Something told me that Edward Wong and "Bob" were not the same guy. Bob was not exactly Chinese-looking. The insurance was listed under a different name—EW Investigations. Same address in Long Beach, though. Mom and I had lived in L.A. for a little while, so I knew Long Beach. It was this sort of crappy town on the south side of Los Angeles. There was a phone number listed on the registration.

I pulled out Mom's cell phone. It had a little bit of charge left. I called the number, and when a man answered, I said, "Is Bob there?"

"Who?"

"Is this Edward Wong?"

There was a brief pause. "Who am I speaking to?" the man said sharply.

If Bob worked for Edward Wong, then presumably he was as dangerous as Bob was. I hung up.

My phone rang immediately. The caller ID showed up as EW Investigations. I guess caller ID cuts both ways. I turned off the phone. I was feeling more and more nauseated by the minute. I put my head in my hands.

After a while something cut into my fit of depression—a car gunning its engine.

I looked up, and there was Brittany Arnett sitting in the front seat of her Mustang, grinning at me. "Hey!" she said. "Get in!"

"Kiss my ass," I said.

Brittany kept grinning at me, showing off her nice straight, white teeth.

"What?"

She flashed something briefly, then hid it behind the door. It looked like a plastic bag. Full of ID cards.

"You didn't think I was *serious* about busting you, Chass?" she said. "God! I was just kidding."

I got up, ran around the car, jumped in the front seat. She tossed the plastic bag in my lap. I yanked it open greedily. Inside were the ID cards her father had showed me over the weekend.

Brittany floored the engine. "Bye-bye, suckers!" she yelled out the window, waving at the kids on the grass. A couple of girls looked up at us sullenly.

"Where you going?" I said.

"What, you think you ought to go to PE instead of figuring out what happened to your mom?"

"Good point. . . ."

"I thought so."

The car hung a right, past a sign out front that said, ATTITUDE NOT APTITUDE DETERMINES ALTITUDE. Mr. Winbush, the assistant principal—everybody called him "The Bush"—was always putting these lame quotes on the sign board, and then kids would come down at night and move the letters around so they'd spell out rude stuff. Apparently somebody had been busy last night, because the other side of the sign said TITTIES ATTUNE TO A DETERMINED DUDE. As we pulled onto the road, I saw the Bush storming out toward the sign, his face all red.

"Yeaaahhhhh!" I screamed. I don't know why, but suddenly I felt a lot better.

Brittany opened the glove box, pulled out a water bottle, popped the topped, squirted a stream of it in her mouth "Thirsty?"

I wasn't really, but she stuck the bottle in my hand, so I squirted some in my mouth too. It burned like gasoline. I started choking.

"Jesus," I said. "What is that?"

"You never had vodka?" she said. "I thought you were little Miss Rock and Roll?"

"That doesn't mean I drink," I said hotly.

"You don't drink? At all?" She seemed amazed.

"No, actually I don't."

"Well, give it back to me then." She took another pull of vodka then tossed the water bottle on the floor. "So who were you talking to on the phone?" she said. "You looked all queer for a minute there."

I shook my head. "Long story."

"I've got nothing but time, girlfriend."

My natural inclination, after all these years with Mom, was to say nothing. But something inside me was ready to talk I guess. We drove around on all these country roads, Brittany sucking occasionally on her vodka bottle while I told her about my life. I told her about how

Mom and I chose our names, how we had our suitcases packed by the door, the whole bit. It just came pouring out, the whole crazy story of my life.

"God!" she said when I finally stopped talking. "You seriously don't know your real name?"

I shook my head.

She drove in silence for a while. Then suddenly she grabbed her cell phone off the dash and said, "What's your cell number?"

I told her.

"Check this out," she said. Then she dialed the number for my phone.

"Why are you calling me?" I said as my phone started ringing.

"Look at your caller ID," she said.

I did. The incoming call line read YALLEE CTY SHERIFF.

"So?" I said.

"One of the perks of Daddy's job, he gets me a cell phone, paid for by the county. Isn't that the coolest?"

I still didn't get it.

"Come on, spit it out. What's the number for this Edward Wong dude, Chass?"

I pulled the envelope out, read off the number. She dialed the number then said, "Is this Edward Wong?"

Her voice sounded different suddenly. Grown up. Authoritative.

"Yes, Mr. Wong," she continued. "This is Sheriff's Detective Sergeant Arnett down here in Yallee County, Alabama. We have just located an abandoned vehicle, a Mercedes, registered to your name. Uh-huh. Yes, sir. No, sir. Well, I need to know why it's here. Is it stolen? Sir? Sir? I'm asking you a question. Is this a company vehicle that's out here being lawfully used by an employee of yours? Or not?"

She winked at me. I had to admit, she was pretty good.

"Mr. Wong, this is a serious matter. If this is some sort of crime scene, I need to secure this vehicle and take it into evidence. It could be several months before you get it back. Uh-*huh*. So is it abandoned? Or not? An employee of yours was using it. I see. Now we're getting somewhere. And what was that employee's name?"

She snapped her fingers at me then made a scribble motion in the air. I dug a pen out of my purse and handed it to her. She wrote something on her hand.

"Very good, sir. We'll just leave it right where it is for your employee to pick up then. Glad to be of service. Yes, sir. You take care now."

She clicked the OFF button on her phone then held out her palm toward me. There in red ink was a name. NILES HENRY.

"That's Bob?" I said.

"Looks like it. This guy got all squirrelly when I

121

started asking about his car. Then I told him we might have to impound it, and he suddenly got a little more forthcoming."

"Man," I said. "You're good."

"I know." She flipped her hair back theatrically, gave me a big smile.

"So Bob or Niles or whatever his name is, is a private investigator," I said. "The big question is, who hired EW Investigations to look into this? You didn't happen to ask, did you?"

"He wouldn't have told me anyway."

"Probably not."

"So you and Ben went back to the car," Brittany said, "and this Niles or Bob or whatever his name is—he was gone."

I nodded.

"If somebody came and got him, this Edward Wong guy should have known about it. Right? Because they'd both be working for Wong. And they'd have gotten the car."

"Stands to reason."

"So he must have crawled into the woods and died," she said. "Or . . ."

"Or he crawled to the road, and somebody picked him up and took him to the hospital."

She handed me her cell phone. "Your turn."

"Huh?" I said.

"I'm driving, I can't be messing around calling every hospital in the area."

I took her phone. After a minute, I dialed. "Hello?" I said. My heart was zipping along in my chest. "This is Sheriff's Investigator Pureheart down here in Yallee County," I said. "I'm trying to find out about a man who's been injured and may have been checked into your hospital. Yes, ma'am. Niles Henry is his name. No?" I paused. "What about somebody who might have been in an accident and they don't know his name. Is that possible?"

I hung up the phone, and a smile spread across my face. He wasn't there, but there were plenty more hospitals around that I could try.

"See?" she said. "It's that easy."

THIRTEEN

THAT NIGHT AFTER supper, Ben and I sat out in the garden behind his house and swatted mosquitoes while I told him what Brittany and I had found out about the guy who'd attacked me. I'd expected him to be excited at what I'd discovered. But instead he seemed to be angry.

"Why are you hanging out with her?" he said when I finished my story. "I wouldn't trust her as far as I could throw her."

"Yeah, but—"

"Yeah but what? I guarantee you she's gonna screw

you. She's probably going home and telling all this stuff to her dad."

"That wouldn't be the worst thing in the world."

"What, that you came in and stole county property? That you, like, encouraged somebody to tamper with evidence of a crime?"

"Why are you getting all bent out of shape?" I said.

He didn't say anything for a minute. "You could have at least called me," he said.

Then it dawned on me. "Oh my God! You're jealous. You're jealous because I have another friend besides you."

"She's not your friend."

"You don't know that."

Ben just looked at me then shook his head sadly, like he was talking to a four-year-old. We sat in silence for a while, listening to the katydids going *scree scree scree* up in the pine trees. Ever since I'd met Ben, I'd felt comfortable around him. It was like it was easier to be me around him than around anybody I'd ever known. Except maybe Mom. But now I felt this odd friction, something I couldn't put my finger on.

Ben's dad was back in the studio welding his sculpture, the door open, the tiny blue-white point of light shedding eerie sparks in the night.

"You know what we have to do," Ben said finally.

I didn't say anything. But I knew too.

"We have to go into that house," he said. "We have to see what's in that basement."

"Uh . . . ," I said.

He looked at me for about a minute. Then a disgusted expression came across his face. "You didn't."

"It was Brittany's suggestion," I said. "Otherwise I would have asked you first."

"What time?"

"Like, one o'clock tonight?"

He sighed. "Her car or mine?"

We were waiting for Brittany at the end of Ben's driveway at one that night. She eased up to the mailbox, her head-lights off, at a couple minutes past the hour. She was wearing a skintight black outfit, and her hair was pulled back in a ponytail like some jewel thief in a movie. I noticed Ben's eyes running down her body as he climbed in.

"Hi, Ben!" she said. Same flirty voice she'd used that morning outside the sheriff's office. She drove at a sedate pace back into town. Thankfully there was no vodka bottle in evidence.

The old Purvis place—that's what I was calling it in my mind now—stood on a very large lot of maybe two or three acres, with ancient oaks ringing the property. The streetlamp nearest the house was dead, and the whole area was nearly lightless. I hadn't noticed it before, but there was a family grave plot behind the house, with old headstones tilted this way and that.

"Okay, this is a little creepy, y'all," Brittany said.

"It's just a house," Ben said. His voice didn't sound so confident though.

We walked slowly toward the front door, tried the handle. It was locked.

"Maybe we should break a window," Brittany said.

An owl hooted. I jumped at the sound, then laughed nervously.

"There's a better way," Ben said. His teeth gleamed in the dim light. He held up a key. "Dad used to live here, you know. He still has keys."

He inserted the key in the lock, twisted, pushed the door open. Inside, the house was pitch-black.

I took out a flashlight and shined it around the room. The place looked just like it had before—lots of ruined old furniture, boxes of junk piled here and there, blotchy paintings of racehorses and hunting dogs on the walls.

"This is *so* cool," Brittany stage-whispered.

"I don't think we have to whisper," Ben said in a loud voice. "There's nobody around here."

Brittany gave him a dirty look but then said, "If you say so, Ben," in a really syrupy way.

"Let's go downstairs," I said. "That's where the banging was coming from."

We wandered around looking for the stairs down to the basement and eventually found them in the kitchen. Just as we were about to go down, I heard a short, low groan from above us.

We all froze. My heart was pounding suddenly.

"What was that?" Brittany was whispering again.

"It's an old house," Ben said. "They settle and make noise." He sounded confident, but his face was nervous.

"Let's get this over with," I said, leading the way down the stairs.

What we found down below us was a large basement excavated from the raw red clay soil. No concrete floor, just bare earth. There wasn't much to see. In one corner was an old furnace. Some rusting tools hung along one wall. The foundations of the house were stone, disappearing down into the dirt.

"It's a hundred and fifty years old," Ben said. "They didn't use brick or concrete much back then."

"Then what's that?" I said. I'd been rotating my flashlight around the room. Three of the walls were soil. But the fourth, caught in the beam of my flashlight, was brick.

"I don't see anything," Brittany said.

Ben frowned, walked over to the wall. There were chunks of brick and mortar littering the dirt next to the wall. "It's brick," he said. "Lots newer than the house."

He knocked on it with the butt of his big aluminum flashlight. It made a hollow bang. He backed up, trained his light on it too.

"There's a whole room behind there," I said.

"Yeah, but where's the door?" Brittany said.

Ben shook his head. "There's not one."

"But why would you make a room if . . ." Brittany let her question hang in the air.

Ben backed up a few steps. "Look," he said. "Some of this mortar is really new. Same for the brick. I think your dad and his men tore a big enough hole in here to see what was inside and then bricked it up again after they were done."

"Why would they do that?" I said.

Ben shrugged.

I turned and walked to the far end of the room, where I pulled a big sledgehammer off the wall. "Well, let's find out," I said. Then I walked over to the wall, lifted the hammer, smashed it against the brick.

Ben blinked. "Are you trippin'? Sombody's gonna hear us."

"I thought you said there was nobody around here," I said.

"Yeah, but . . ."

I brought the hammer up again, smashed it against the wall. Nothing happened, other than a few tiny chips of brick flying off and hitting me in the leg. "Ow," I said.

"Chass, we're gonna get in big trouble," Ben said.

"What, you're chicken?" Brittany said lightly.

"No but . . ."

I hammered the wall again. Still nothing.

"Oh for godsake," Ben said finally. "Here." He took the hammer, held it more like a golf club, and started pounding methodically at knee level. Ben looked at ease with the big hammer. He'd done a lot of work for his father out in the sculpture workshop, and was good with tools. Within a minute, he'd knocked four or five bricks out. From there it got easier. Pretty soon there was a hole big enough to crawl through.

I pushed him aside, pointed my flash into the hole.

"What do you see?" Brittany said.

I saw a room, no more than ten feet square, with a dirt floor. It was stone empty. I felt a wave of disappointment.

"Nothing," I said.

"Let's go in!" Brittany said.

"Why?" Ben said. "There's nothing there."

"Let's go in anyway." Brittany grabbed Ben's flashlight and crawled through the hole. Ben looked at me questioningly. I shrugged. He followed, and then I came in after.

"Well," I said. "Here we are."

There was no more to see inside than out. A few spiderwebs, a red dirt floor covered with a dusting of gray mold. There were boot prints in the mold, prints from the sheriff's deputies I assumed.

"Okay, here's my guess," I said. "Mom came down here to look for something. She started breaking a hole in the wall. Somebody interrupted her before she got very far. When Brittany's dad got down here, he found the hole, so he had his men enlarge it. They came in, looked around, found nothing."

"So they bricked the hole back up," Ben finished.

"Exactly."

"Well, there's obviously nothing here," Ben said.

Suddenly Brittany looked nervous. "Wait." She held a finger over her lips.

"What?"

"Shhh."

We stood in silence.

"Did you hear that?" she said.

"Hear what?"

Suddenly there was a hollow boom that reverberated around the tiny room.

"What the—!" Ben said.

Another boom.

"It's right outside," Brittany whispered.

BOOM. This time louder.

"Ohmygod." Brittany grabbed Ben's arm. Ben was looking panicky.

"Turn off the flashlights," he said.

BOOOM!

My heart must have been doing two hundred beats a minute.

"Hold me, Ben," Brittany said.

BOOOMM!!!

"Let's get the hell out of here," I whispered.

"It's too dark," Ben said.

I turned my flash back on—

—just in time to see Brittany kick the wall behind her.

BOOOOMMM!!!!

It took me a second to make the connection. But then I saw it: it had just been Brittany, Brittany the whole time, kicking the wall.

Brittany started laughing like a maniac. "I got y'all!" she said, "I got y'all *so* good."

Ben still had his arm tight around her shoulder.

"You could probably let go now, Ben," she said.

"Brittany, you suck!" I said. But I couldn't help laughing.

Then we were all doubled over, the release from fear so strong that after a minute we were practically panting.

As I was bent over laughing I noticed something. It was a subtle thing, but the floor below us wasn't even. I stopped laughing very suddenly.

After a minute Ben noticed me staring at the floor. He stopped laughing. Brittany stopped too.

"What?" Ben said.

I pointed my flashlight at the ground. In the far corner of the little room was a place where the soil was just a little higher than the surrounding dirt. It was no more than a couple or three inches higher, so subtle that you could only see it when the flashlight was at knee level. Like I'd been holding it when I had been doubled over laughing.

"Six feet long," I said.

Brittany made a sharp intake of breath.

I climbed out of the hole, grabbed a rusty old shovel off the wall, and walked over to the raised piece of soil. In this part of Alabama, the soil is a red clay, not blood-red exactly, but a creepy color if you're not used to it.

"You know what?" Brittany said. "I think maybe I changed my mind. Let's go."

"Shine your light where I'm digging," I said.

"I'll dig," Ben said.

"Just shine your light." I kept digging. It didn't take long. Pretty soon I heard a soft crunch, felt my shovel hit something. I started digging more carefully. And pretty soon there it was, clear as a bell.

I stepped back. In the pale, dim light of the flashlight beam, about a foot beneath the surface of the floor, lay a human skull.

FOURTEEN

"WELL I GUESS we know what happened to Nancy Rydel," I said.

Brittany squinted curiously at me. "Nancy who?"

I hadn't told her that part of the story. I'd just told her about Mom disappearing from the house here. I didn't necessarily want to get into the Nancy Rydel thing with her. Not yet. After all, her dad may have had something to do with Nancy Rydel's disappearance.

Ben looked at me sharply, then said, "Nothing."

"Just an inside joke."

"Well now doesn't seem like the time for being funny."

We stared at the skull some more. "What do we do?" Ben said.

While we were thinking, the room was silent. Then we heard something. A soft, shuffling sound.

"That's not funny, Brittany," I said.

"It's not me," Brittany whispered.

The sound, again. It was definitely coming from outside the little room. Somewhere upstairs.

I shined my light on Brittany's face. She looked genuinely terrified. Ben grabbed the shovel from me, holding it over his shoulder like an ax.

"It's just the house settling," Ben said. But now he was whispering too. . . .

"Then why are you holding that shovel like you're about to bash somebody's head in?" I whispered back.

Silence. I felt shaky with fear.

Then another sound—this time terrifyingly identifiable. Footsteps. Soft, careful, purposeful—but clearly footsteps, the floor creaking above us.

"*Oh* hell," Ben said. "Let's bail!"

Then we were climbing out the hole, thundering up the stairs.

"The back door, the back door, the *back* door!" I yelled.

Then we were in the kitchen. I heard someone behind us yelling, "Stop!"

I led the way toward the back door. It was locked. Ben tried the handle. The footsteps were hammering toward us down the hallway.

Ben smashed the door open with his shoulder. He was still carrying the shovel in his hand.

"Out!" Ben yelled.

Brittany didn't need any urging. She was through the door in a flash. I followed her. Over my shoulder I saw Ben hurl the shovel at someone. There was a crash and a howl of pain, and then we were pounding down a path, through the tipsy-looking gravestones. Behind us a man was running toward us. In the dark I couldn't see his face.

Then we were in Brittany's car, tearing down the road. The man burst onto the street behind us, face shrouded in darkness, yelling something I couldn't make out over the roar of the Mustang's big engine.

After driving for about three minutes, we reached the edge of town. There were no headlights in the rearview mirror, nobody following us.

Brittany suddenly pulled the car over to the side of the road and stopped. She held her hands up in front of her face. They were trembling like leaves.

"Okay," she said almost wonderingly. "Was that the coolest thing ever? Or what?"

FIFTEEN

THE NEXT MORNING, still no note in the classified section of the newspaper for me. Nothing to indicate Mom was still alive.

A few minutes later, as Ben and I were going out to the Batmobile to drive to school, we heard a horn honk. We turned around and saw Brittany's green Mustang barreling up the dirt driveway, a cloud of dust rising behind it.

"Hey, y'all!" she yelled out the window.

"What's *she* want?" Ben said.

"Need a ride?" she said.

"I have a car," Ben said.

"Oh, come on!" Brittany said.

Ben looked at me. I shrugged, and we got in.

"So did y'all sleep at all?" Brittany said.

I shook my head. "Not much."

"I kept thinking about that skull. All night."

I didn't say anything.

"We got to tell my dad," she said. "Y'all know that, don't you?"

Ben looked at me questioningly. I shook my head slightly. "Brittany," I said, "he's the last person we need to tell."

"What are you talking about?" she said.

"Just trust me on this," I said.

She turned out onto the road and started heading for town—the opposite direction from the school.

"Where are you going?" I said.

"Uh . . . ," she said.

"Aw man!" Ben said. "You told your dad already. Didn't you?"

"Uh . . . ," she said again.

"See?" Ben said disgustedly to me. "What did I tell you?"

"She didn't know," I said.

"Didn't know what?" Brittany said.

"Never mind."

"I didn't even tell him what we found!" Brittany said hotly. "I just told him we found *something*."

Brittany pulled up in front of the old Purvis house. A sheriff's department cruiser was parked out front next to the sheriff's personal car. Brittany's father was leaning up against his car, a deputy standing next to him with a shovel. "So you kids broke into an old house and vandalized it?" Sheriff Arnett said. "I could lock y'all up and send you to juvie if I felt like it."

"It's my family's house," Ben said sullenly.

"Not anymore," the sheriff said. "The county seized it for nonpayment of taxes."

"You ought to be *glad* about what we did, Daddy," Brittany said. "It's like a public service or something."

"Just show me whatever mysterious thing you found," her father said.

We went into the house and down into the cellar. Sheriff Arnett pointed at the wall, his face furious. "You did this? You broke this wall?"

"So?" Brittany said.

"That's two felonies. Destruction of private property. Breaking and entering." He walked over to the wall, pointed his flashlight in, then turned to us. "Well?" he said. "What's the big mystery here?"

Ben and I looked at each other and shrugged. Brittany walked over to the wall, stared into the little room, then turned to us with wide eyes. "Y'all! Look! It's gone!"

"What's gone?" Sheriff Arnett said. "All I see is a hole."

"Daddy, there was a body in here yesterday."

"Brittany, as of this moment you are grounded," her father said. "I'm tired of listening to you making up stories."

I edged forward and peered over her shoulder. The sheriff was right. In the place where we had left a small hole with a skull in the bottom of it, there was now a large hole, just long enough to fit a body in. But there was no body.

"Very funny, kids," Sheriff Arnett said. "You broke into a house, you vandalized county property, you dug your little hole to look like somebody was buried here, you wasted my time and Deputy Anderson's time—very, very cute. I hope you're proud of yourselves."

"But, Daddy—"

"Zip it, Brittany. You go upstairs and wait in your car."

"But—"

"Now!"

Brittany slunk up the stairs.

"Ben," the sheriff said. "I know your daddy didn't teach you to act this way."

"No, sir," Ben said.

"And you, young lady . . ." He pointed his finger at me. "You stay away from my daughter."

"Me? Stay away from her?" I said. "She was the one who—"

"Ben, you go upstairs too. Deputy Anderson, make sure he gets to the car."

"Yes, sir."

Ben and the big deputy clumped up the stairs.

I could see little beads of sweat on Sheriff Arnett's upper lip. His neat hair gleamed in the dim light. "Turn around," he said softly.

"Excuse me?"

"Turn around, face the wall."

"What—"

"I'm not asking you again, girl."

I turned and faced the wall.

"Both hands behind you."

I did as I was told. The sheriff snapped a pair of cuffs on me, tightened them so hard that I winced.

"You like that?" he said. "You like the feel of that?"

"Please . . ."

He shoved my face against the wall, leaned close to my ear so I could smell his minty breath. "I don't know what game you're playing. But it ends here."

"Sir, I'm not playing a game. I just want to find my mother."

"I ran your name through the system. Your mother's too. It seems y'all don't exist."

I could feel him breathing against me.

"What's your real name?"

I didn't say anything. What would have been the point?

"I asked you a question. What's your name?"

I almost felt like laughing. I was so scared, I'd have told him anything. But he'd asked the one question I didn't have an answer for.

"I know you stole those ID cards," he said to me.

"What?"

"Spare me the innocent act. Deputy Anderson saw you rifling through my desk."

I knew there was no point in telling him it was his darling daughter who'd done it. It would only make him madder.

"I'm placing you under arrest for obstruction of justice and tampering with evidence," he said.

"Did *you* dig her up?" I said.

"Dig who up?"

"Nancy Rydel. You know that's who we found in there," I said.

The room was silent for a long time.

"Go ahead, Sheriff, lock me up. But if you do, I'm going to tell the Alabama state police about who was in that grave. Even if they never find her, you know what, I don't think it's a subject you want getting dredged up again."

The sheriff didn't say anything for a long time. Finally I heard a jingle of keys, then the sheriff unlocked the cuffs. I felt blood rush into my hands.

"Young lady, I'm in a good mood, so I'm gonna forget about this whole thing," the sheriff said. "But I want those ID cards back. Failing that, I *will* lock you up and put you in the juvie system. And God help you then, little girl."

"Thank you, sir."

"Something tells me this isn't the last time you're going to be wearing these," he said, pulling the cuffs off my wrists. "Your kind gets used to it."

"*My* kind? What kind is that, sir?" I said.

"Trash," he said. "Nameless, faceless, worthless trash, blowing in on one ill wind and blowing out on another."

Ben and I drove to school in silence, riding in the backseat of the deputy's cruiser. There were no handles in the back. For us to get out, the deputy had to open the doors.

The stoners on the smoking ramp were watching us as we drove up.

"Busted!" one kid yelled.

144

"Look out! It's America's most *un*wanted!" another one said.

All the burnouts on the smoking ramp thought they were pretty funny.

"I guess we better forget about this whole thing," Ben said sullenly. "We're just going to get in trouble."

"In *trouble*!" I said. "My mom is missing, and I'm three days away from going into foster care. How much more in trouble can I get in?"

"The sheriff said he'd arrest me if I did anything else," Ben said. "It could go on my permanent record."

"Oh. Your permanent record. *Well* then." I walked away shaking my head and feeling very alone.

After lunch I went to the library and logged on to a computer. I took out the ID cards Brittany had stolen from her father's desk and laid them down in a row.

There were six of them. I rearranged them, putting them in chronological order.

The newest one was very recent, only about four months old—a company ID for something called the Elmwood Group showing Mom's picture with the name Joyce Rodgers under it. Next was an Alaska driver's license with the name Joan Allen. Then a military ID with the name of Gillian Oberdorf. Then a bank card for a Mavis Blouin. Then a couple of driver's licenses from

Maryland and Kentucky. And the last one was a back-stage pass for Madison Square Garden in New York. Unlike the others, which were plastic, it was made from heavy paper. It was dated sixteen or seventeen years back and was brittle with age. The name on it was Jenna Farmer.

I started searching the Internet for the names. There were a fair number of matches, but none that seemed useful, so I looked up the Elmwood Group. I found that it was a company that did entertainment consulting—whatever that was—and that it was a subsidiary of Apex Global Media Corporation.

I searched the Web site for Joyce Rodgers. It turned out that Joyce Rodgers did, in fact, exist. She was an entertainment lawyer for the company and ran their office in Birmingham. Which wasn't forty-five minutes from High Hopes. They had photos of all their branch heads on the site, so I pulled up Joyce Rodgers. She was about fifty years old, with gray hair and glasses, and probably weighed about two-fifty. Definitely not my mom.

I searched the Web for Joan Allen—the name from ID number two—and the Elmwood Group. No matches. I tried Joan Allen and Apex Global Media.

Bam. Joan Allen worked in accounting for Apex Global Media Corporation in Columbus, Ohio. Or at least she had when the Web site was put up three years ago. Three years ago was when we moved down here from Columbus.

I ran the next name. Gillian Oberdorf. In addition to serving in the Army Reserve, she was a shipping clerk with Pro-Max Distribution. A subsidiary of Apex Global Media in Moline, Illinois.

I felt the skin crawl on the back of my neck. Moline was the town we'd lived in before moving to Columbus, Ohio. What was the deal with Apex Global Media?

I ran the next three names, but nothing popped up. Maybe they were so old that the connections between the names and Apex had disappeared from the Web. Or maybe they just weren't there to begin with.

It was strange. What was Mom's connection to Apex? Why had she found these Apex connections in every town we'd moved to? After all, we moved randomly. Each time we moved, she closed her eyes and poked the map with her finger. And wherever her finger landed, that's where we went.

But then something occurred to me. What if it *wasn't* random? What if Mom had been moving to each place intentionally? What if the whole eyes-closed/finger-on-the-map thing was a charade designed to make it seem as though we were moving to each new town by accident? All she'd have to do was peek, keep her eyes half open. . . .

It gave me the creeps just thinking about it. Had Mom been working some kind of plan all these years?

I looked up Apex Global Media Corporation.

Their Web site had a list of their divisions—Magazines, Publishing, Film, Music. It was a huge company worth billions of dollars. I kept surfing around the Web site. It was mostly boring junk like why the company was such a good investment and everything. I was about to flip past the page that said LETTER FROM THE PRESIDENT at the top. But then, suddenly, I stopped.

At the end of the boring letter about acquisitions and profits and all this crap, it had the signature of the president of the company, along with a big smiling picture of this cheesy-looking bald guy in a suit. His name was Kyle Van Epps. I stared at the name. Where had I seen it before? I felt sure that I'd seen it. Then I remembered. I immediately picked up my cell phone and dialed the number for the city library.

"Circulation, this is Mr. Percival. How can I help you?"

"Hi, this is Chass Pureheart," I said. "The girl that was doing research about Jimmy Laws?"

"Oh, hi!" he said.

"Yeah, I was wondering . . ." I told him what I was trying to find out.

As I was talking, my biology teacher, Miss Turner,

walked by. She looked over at me and glared. "Young lady, you know better than to use your cell phone at school."

On the other end of the line, Mr. Percival, the library guy, said, "One second, Chass, I'll check on that."

"Yes, ma'am," I said to the teacher as Mr. Percival put me on hold.

I set the phone down like I had turned it off. Miss Turner raised her eyebrows. "I saw that!" she said.

"Huh?" I said innocently.

"I saw you didn't turn it off. You think I'm just going to walk away and then you can carry on with all your little chitchat-chitchat? Hm? Hm?"

"No, ma'am," I said innocently.

She pointed at the phone, snapped her fingers.

"Huh?"

"Give me the phone, Chass! Now."

Coming out of the phone I could hear a tiny voice. "Chass? Chass?"

I held up one finger to Miss Turner. "I'm doing research for my history report," I said.

"Oh, yeah, right." Miss Turner was dripping sarcasm.

"Chass? Hello?" Mr. Percival's tiny voice.

"I swear, Miss Turner!" I picked up the phone. "Mr. Percival?"

"I found that name," the librarian said.

"Great."

Miss Turner tried to snatch the phone away from me. I jerked my head away.

"You wanted to know the name of the record company executive whose boat Jimmy Laws was in when he drowned? It's right here."

Miss Turner was a large woman, with thick fingers tipped by heavy red-painted fingernails. She grabbed hold of the phone, catching my ear with one of her nails, started yanking on the phone. I grabbed it with both hands, hanging on for dear life while she was impaling my ear with her nail. "Young lady as soon as I get this phone, you're going straight to the principal's office!"

Mr. Percival began reading while Miss Turner was giving me whiplash, jerking my head around. "'Today two men drowned in Long Island Sound on the boat of a prominent music industry executive,' it says. 'Found dead in the water were recording artist Jimmy Laws, thirty-one, beloved by teen fans for his tortured love songs, along with twenty-nine-year-old recording engineer—'"

"Could we kind of cut to the chase?" I said. "The name. The name."

"Young lady! You. Give. Me. That. Phone. This. *Minute*!" My head was practically knocking into the sides of the carrel I was sitting in by now.

"Sure, sure, Chass," Mr. Percival said. "The boat was owned by, let's see his name is—"

Miss Turner finally got the phone, held it up triumphantly. "You're not going to win a tug-of-war with me, Chass," she said grimly. "Now you get up to Mr. Winbush's office this instant."

I made a grab for the phone, yanked it out of her hand, started running through the library, dodging around the tables full of kids doing book reports. Miss Turner came bulling after me. The kids were staring wide-eyed.

"Could you give me that name again, Mr. Percival?" I shouted as I ran.

"Jimmy Laws died on a boat owned by—"

Whatever he said, I missed it because at that exact moment Miss Turner tackled me like she was playing defensive end for the Crimson Tide. She was unbelievably fast for an old fat lady. I crashed into the wall and fell down. The phone fell out of my hand, hit a shelf of books, bounced twice. I wondered if it was broken. It was lying about three inches from my face.

"What?" I said. "Could you say that again, Mr. Percival?"

We lay there on the stinky indoor-outdoor carpet, breathing hard. I could feel Miss Turner's body pressing down on me.

The phone lay on the ground next to us. But I could still make out Mr. Percival's tiny little voice. "—Van Epps. I said, Kyle Van Epps."

Miss Turner grabbed the phone, stabbed the OFF button. "Hah!" she said.

"I think I'm bleeding," I said.

SIXTEEN

THE BUSH GAVE me three days of detention hall, then wrote me out a hall pass to go back to sixth period.

As I was walking back toward the gym, I heard somebody go, "Pssst."

I turned and looked. It was Brandi Chun, poking her head furtively out of a classroom. "Hey," she whispered. "Hey! Where you going?"

"Gym," I said. Brandi Chun was the cocaptain of the junior varsity cheerleading squad and a good buddy of Brittany's. I don't think she had ever spoken to me in her life.

Brandi glanced over her shoulder, like she was making sure the teacher wasn't looking, then looked back at me. "I heard you got in a fight with Miss Turner. That is *way* cool."

"It wasn't a fight," I said.

"So," she whispered, "Brittany's looking for you."

"Why?"

"I don't know."

"She said meet her on the smoking ramp after school."

"Uh. Okay."

"You are like my *hero*, girl!" she said. "So Brittany's telling everybody about your big concert on Friday. I want to come."

"Concert? Oh. Well unfortunately it's at a bar," I said.

"I heard you could hook me up with a fake ID," she said.

"Where'd you hear that?"

"Brandi!" I could hear Mr. Sherman's voice. "What do you think you're doing?"

"Nothing, sir!" Brandi said in a big fake innocent voice. She winked at me. "You rock, girl!"

Then she closed the door. The second snobbiest girl in High Hopes telling me I was her hero. Go figure.

• • •

After the bell rang, I went outside and saw Ben standing in line by one of the buses. "Hey," I said. "Come with me."

"What's up?"

"I think Brittany can give us a ride."

"You *think*?"

I shrugged.

"If I miss the bus," Ben said, "I'll have to call Dad, and he'll give me a raft of crap."

"Oh, come on."

He scowled then followed me over to the smoking ramp.

As we walked over, one of the stoners—this kid named Jay-Jay Brice—said, "Rock and roll, Chass!"

"Huh?" I said.

"Friday night!" he said. "It's *on*, dude!" He threw me this sort of gang sign-looking thing with his fingers, like all the stoners did when they went to Ozzy Osbourne concerts, then threw his cigarette butt on the ground and walked off.

Brittany was now standing alone on the smoking ramp, sucking on a Marlboro Light. "Hi, Ben!" She always said it the same way when she saw him now, like she was about to go into the makeout room at a party with him. Only sort of joking. Like she was half making fun of him and half not.

"So let's go to Birmingham," she said.

"What?"

"Birmingham. Isn't that where the hospital is? The one where the guy who tried to kill you is staying?"

"I've got detention hall," I said.

"Blow it off. Come to Birmingham."

"Are you crazy," Ben said. "I can't go to Birmingham!" He turned and started walking away. "I'm taking the bus."

He headed across the parking lot, but by the time he got there, his bus was starting to pull out. He began to run, an awkward thing with the big stack of books in his backpack. Kids leaned out the windows and started hooting at him. "Run faster!" "Ah hah hah!" "Run, Ben, you big freak!" And so on.

The bus didn't even slow down.

"Dammit!" Ben threw his books on the ground and kicked them.

Brittany dropped her cigarette on the concrete, stepped on it. "Guess he's coming to Birmingham after all," she said.

"I thought your dad said you were grounded," I said.

"What's he gonna do?" she said. "Arrest me?"

It took us forty-five minutes to get to Birmingham. As we rolled into the parking lot of University Hospital, Ben said, "So explain to me again how you know this guy is here?"

"I called around and said I was with the sheriff's department," I said. "I just asked if a criminal suspect named Niles Henry had checked in. Turned out he hadn't. But one of the people I talked to said, 'Are you sure you're not looking for a John Doe?' I go, 'Well, maybe.' I didn't really know what she was talking about. So she's like 'Yeah, we had this guy come in the other day, apparently got hit by a car. But he didn't have any identification and wouldn't give his name. That might be your guy. He's in room three twenty-seven.'"

Ben nodded vaguely. He had been sprawled in the back of Brittany's Mustang looking unhappy since we left school. "And we're planning on doing—what? Asking the guy why he wanted to kill you?"

"I don't know," I said. "Maybe."

We got out, went inside the big building, and took the elevator up to the third floor. Brittany got off the elevator first, then stopped wide-eyed.

"What?" I said.

"What the—" Ben pointed.

There at the end of the hallway was Brittany's father. He was walking into a room in the direction of the arrow pointing to 327.

Brittany grabbed both our arms and shoved us back into the elevator. "Daddy will *kill* me if he sees me here!" she said. "Let's *go*!"

It didn't take much urging. We pressed the CLOSE DOOR button and rode back down to the lobby.

"What's your dad doing here?" I said.

"Was that Niles Henry's room?" Ben said.

Brittany shook her head. "I don't know. I don't know."

"Let's just go home," Ben said.

"Ben, why are you being so chicken?" I said. "Let's just wait a couple minutes. We'll go across the street, find a McDonald's or something, grab a Coke, come back, your dad will be gone."

"No, Ben's right," Brittany said, leaning toward him a little. "We gotta go. Daddy told me he'd take my car away if he saw me with y'all again."

"Hey!" I said. "You guys can chicken out if you want. I say we came all the way up here, let's stick around."

Brittany and Ben looked at each other. Ben shrugged. Brittany shrugged. I started crossing the street. I could tell they weren't following me.

I got about halfway across the street when I was suddenly hit by this wave of loneliness. Ben was pretty much all I had in the world right now. And here he was, going off with this bitchy cheerleader instead of following me. I stopped in the middle of the road, hearing their footsteps going in the other direction. But I couldn't make myself turn around and go back. I don't know if it was my natural stubbornness or whether it was just because I had more at stake than they did.

A car threw on its brakes, honked at me. I ran the rest of the way across the street and down the block to McDonald's.

I never looked back.

When I got to McDonald's, the smell of grease wafted down from a vent on the side of the building. Something about it made me feel nauseated. So I stood there, trying to think what I should do.

That's when something struck me. If I was going to play at Ronnie's on Friday, I was going to need a fake ID to prove I was old enough to be in a bar. The owner had told me specifically that he would check my ID.

Every time Mom and I moved, we had to get fake identification—or at least Mom did. And when we moved to High Hopes, I remembered we'd driven up to Birmingham so that she could get a bogus driver's license. Where had she bought it, though?

It was a copy shop, I remembered, in some ugly industrial area over on the other side of the University of Alabama at Birmingham. Which wasn't that far a walk from where I was. If I could just remember where it was located. . . .

I started walking west, and pretty soon I'd gotten into this kind of spooky, half-deserted-looking area. As I was walking along, I saw a black SUV with heavily tinted windows pull up next to me, slow for a moment as though someone inside were staring at me, then ease off down the street.

There were all these big, low warehouses around me now situated on wide streets that not much of anybody seemed to be driving on. I walked through an echoing underpass under the interstate, wandered around a while, and realized I had absolutely no idea where I was going.

I walked a couple more blocks. The black SUV—or one that looked a lot like it—drove by again. I figured it was probably nothing. But still—after what I'd been through this week, I had good reason for being a little paranoid.

The area rapidly got a lot crummier-looking—buildings boarded up, shiftless-looking guys standing around smoking cigarettes, mom-and-pop stores with bars over the windows. Just when I had decided it was high time to turn around and start walking back, I spotted a sign. KEN'S COPY SHOP.

That was it! Ken's—the place Mom got her IDs from. A young black guy was standing out front wearing a baggy Sean John jacket and very dark shades, talking on his cell phone. He was leaned up against a pimped-out old car with huge chrome rims, deafening music shaking the windows. As I got closer, I could tell he was watching me carefully. I knew I was out of place in this neighborhood, but I figured if I could make it inside the copy shop, I'd be fine.

"What up, girl," the guy next to the car said.

I didn't meet his eyes, just kept walking.

"Nah, nah, nah! Don't be all hard-to-get and everything!" he said. There was something both playful and vaguely menacing about him.

My heart was racing as I walked up to the copy shop. Then I felt sick. The place had a sign on the front that said CLOSED. I looked through the dingy glass. The inside had been stripped bare.

"Dammit," I said.

"Mm-*mmm*!" the guy behind me said. I could see him reflected in the glass, looking over the top of his shades at my butt.

I turned around, started walking away. Somehow the guy in the Sean John jacket managed to position himself in exactly the right place so that I had to step into the street to get around him.

"Baby, you in kind of the wrong neighborhood, huh?" he said.

I shrugged, tried to step around him. But he moved a little to his right, cut me off again.

"Yo!" he said. "You in a hurry or something?"

"Something like that."

He looked me up and down. "You a student at the university?" he said.

"You mind letting me by?"

"See, looking at you, I'm thinking maybe you a freshman, sophomore at most, can't get into all the cool clubs, am I right?"

I looked him right in the face. "Step off," I said.

He didn't move. "I mean they got all kind of copy shops over near the university, if you just looking to print out a term paper, something like that. Me, I'm asking myself, why you coming all the way over here just to find a copy shop?"

I glared at him.

"You looking for Ken, baby. Am I right? Hm? Some of them special services he provide? Special ID cards for special people?"

I hesitated. "Maybe."

He grinned, showing off large square teeth. "Ah! Sad thing. My boy Ken—he passed away last year. Something in his brain went pop, and my boy, he just out like a light."

"Well, I guess I better get moving then." In the distance I saw the black SUV ease around the corner, drive by, stop, park at the curb a few blocks away.

"Yeah, see, what it is, Ken had all that equipment? You know what I'm talking about? One of the fellows in the neighborhood helped hisself to all that equipment. Now he in the same line of bidness as Ken."

"Yeah. Who would that be?"

He put out his hand. "Dwayne Crooks, freelance entrepreneur, at your service."

I looked over his shoulder. The black SUV with the dark windows was still sitting there. Probably nothing. But still. It made me not so eager to go back that way just yet. I shook Dwayne's hand.

"What's your name? Come on, I told you mine. Now you holding out on me."

"Chastity."

"Chastity!" His eyebrows went up comically. "You get the wrong body for a name like that. You gonna get the fellows all hot and bothered."

I didn't say anything.

He laughed. "What you need, baby? Driver's license? Food stamp card? Pilot's license? I'll hook up."

"How much?"

He looked me up and down again. "Special price. For you? Two hundred fifty bucks."

My eyes widened. "Two hundred fifty bucks!"

He licked his lips, looked off in the distance. "How much you got?"

"Forty bucks."

He laughed like I was an idiot. "My equipment, this stuff is real high-end. Real sophisticated. You want a cheap-ass Kentucky driver's license, don't have no holograms, no security features? Hey, sure, forty bucks, buy it on the Internet. You come to Dwayne, baby, you looking for the *good* stuff."

"I don't know what you mean."

He opened his wallet, took out two driver's licenses. One said Dwayne Crooks on it. The other said Odell Birdsong. Otherwise they were identical. Same picture, same everything. "See, back in the day, you could print you a license on a color copier, laminate that sucker, couldn't nobody tell it from a real one. Not no more. Like your Alabama vehicle operator's license? Got *all* kind of security features. Got a hologram. Got the state seal superimposed on the photo. Got the photo itself. Even got a biometric ID stripe on the back with your fingerprint coded on it! You think any old copy shop can crank one of these out?"

I shook my head. "Probably not."

"My boy, Ken, he left me like sixty-five thousand dollars' worth of equipment. That's what it takes to do one of these. But when you done, that ID is flawless. See, me, I confess freely to you, I've had me a couple run-ins with the civil authorities. But my cousin Odell? He a deacon down at the Baptist church. So what I do? Mr. Five-oh gets up close and personal with me, I hand him this here ID. The police, he run it through the computer, then he smile at me, sorry for the inconvenience Mr. Birdsong, send me on my merry way. That's what you get for your two fifty. Au-then-*ticity*!"

"That's nice, but I still only have forty dollars."

He looked me up and down for about the tenth time, then he said, "Hop in my ride, baby, I'm feeling a soft spot in my heart for you."

I stood there for a minute feeling like I was in way, way, way over my head. But sometimes when you get in a certain distance, the only way out is to keep moving forward.

"All right," I said.

We drove six or eight blocks with some old school rap blasting so loud I thought my eardrums would bleed, went around a corner, stopped by a chain-link fence. Dwayne hopped out.

"This way to my humble abode," he said, pointing at the fence.

"What, you have to climb a fence to get into your own house?"

"Nah nah nah! It's a hole right there. Just crawl through."

Then I saw it, a place where the fence had been cut and kind of rolled up so you could just squeeze through.

This was getting worse all the time. But now I didn't even know how to get back to the hospital.

Dwayne squeezed through gingerly, taking care not to rip a hole in his fancy leather jacket. "You coming, baby?"

Once again I gave some thought to running. But I guess I just didn't want to look like a chicken. I squeezed through, followed Dwayne down a narrow, stinking alley and through a rusting metal door with a padlock on it.

On the other side of the door was a neat, nicely furnished little apartment. It had black leather furniture, African-looking artwork on the walls, some potted plants in the corner.

"My crib," he said with a wave of his hand as we walked through his living room. On the far side of the room was another door, which he unlocked with an unusually large key. We went through the door and into a room that smelled of chemicals so strongly that it made my eyes water. A number of gleaming machines were lined up along the far wall.

After I came through the door, he locked it behind me, then shot a bolt about the size of a banana. "You want a drink, baby?" he said. "Vodka tonic? Glass of chablis?"

"I don't drink," I said.

He looked at me curiously. "You don't drink, then why come you getting a fake ID?"

"Do I ask you about your business?" I said.

He looked at me for a long time, then said, "You got more going on than you look like you got," he said.

I took out the forty dollars, set it on top of a table by the door. "Let's just get this done," I said.

"See, I'm trying to be friendly and—"

"I didn't come here to make friends."

Something scary flickered across his face for a moment, then he covered it up with a smile. "Then step to the yellow line, baby, we get a picture of you."

I stepped to a line on the floor where he was pointing and he took a flash photo of me. Then he stepped over to a computer. "Need your address and date of birth."

"I don't think so," I said. I didn't want this guy knowing where I lived.

"Baby, can't nobody make a fake driver's license, they don't put all their personal information on it."

I flushed. "Oh, yeah, okay." I told him my address, and he typed it rapidly into the computer.

"Full name?"

"Chastity Pureheart."

He looked up, pulled his sunglasses down on his nose so that for the first time I could see his eyes. They were bloodshot, moist. "Hold on, hold on, hold on. I knew you favored somebody. You related to *Allison* Pureheart?"

"She's my mom."

He rubbed his face. "So she referred you to me."

I nodded. "Sort of."

"Why you didn't say so? Shoot, baby, I got her order waiting."

"Her order?"

"Yeah, she ordered a couple ID cards from me. Very special items. Prepaid for them."

"Oh, yeah, sure. Right, I forgot. She wanted me to pick them up."

He looked at me for a minute. "Forty dollars, I was gonna give you my standard Kentucky license, got no security features on it. But since you Allison's baby girl, I'ma give you a Alabama license—much more complicated—got all the biometrics and everything."

Fifteen minutes later Dwayne Crooks handed me an envelope that contained not only a new ID that said I was twenty-one years old, but also two ID cards with my mother's pictures on them. I didn't want to make a big thing out of it, so I took them without looking at them.

We were walking out of the building toward the chain-link fence with the hole cut in it when I stopped. There it was again. Parked across the street from me was a black SUV with tinted windows.

I stopped.

"What?" Dwayne said.

"That SUV over there. You ever see it in the neighborhood?"

Dwayne looked at it. "Should I have?"

"I don't know."

Dwayne looked at me for a minute. "What you into, girl? You all a sudden making me nervous."

I stood without moving. Across the street the door to the black SUV opened and an unusually tall Asian guy in a long black coat started walking toward us. He had something black and metallic in his hand.

Dwayne spotted the man, grabbed my arm, and propelled me back toward his apartment, through the door. He locked it behind him, then went into the next room, locked that door too.

I could hear my breath coming hard and ragged. Dwayne suddenly had a sheen of sweat on his face. "Who that dude is?" he demanded.

"I don't know."

Dwayne looked like he was thinking. Finally he seemed to come to a decision. "I'ma have to take matters in hand," he said. "Then I'ma deal with you." He pointed his finger at me, set his car keys on the table, then walked out the door and closed it.

I heard something outside, a few angry words, a scraping noise, then two sharp bangs. Gunshots, I was sure of it. I ran over, shot the bolt home on the door to the room with the equipment in it, then grabbed Dwayne's keys and locked it. Within seconds, someone was pounding on the door.

"Dwayne?" I yelled. "Dwayne?"

"Dwayne's otherwise occupied," a voice on the other side of the door said. The voice was calm and unhurried. "Open up, Chastity. We need to talk."

I froze.

"I'm not here to hurt you, sweetheart. I'm your friend."

For a moment I didn't hear anything else. Then someone began pounding on the door. Not like they were knocking with their knuckles. It was like they were smashing it with an ax or a sledgehammer.

I looked frantically around the room. I couldn't see anywhere to go. No doors, no windows. Then I saw something—a tiny plywood door behind one of the big pieces of printing equipment. I squeezed behind the printing machine, pried the plywood cover off with Dwayne's keys, and then crawled through the little door. Apparently Dwayne had made himself an escape hatch in case the police ever raided his underground printing business. I found myself in a brick basement, almost completely dark. I ran through it, found some stairs, ran up them, pushed open a door, and found myself outside in a deserted yard surrounded by a barbed-wire fence. It took me about thirty seconds to find a hole cut in this fence. I squeezed through, gouging my arms and legs on the steel wire. Behind me I heard footsteps.

"Come on, I just want to talk."

The big Asian guy was still trying to push his way through the hole in the fence when I got to Dwayne's car. I fired it up with his keys, hung a U-turn, and drove furiously down the road. I didn't even have my learner's permit yet, so it was sort of like, *learn to drive in one easy lesson*. Step one, guy with gun comes after you. Step two, floor it. Step three, try not to smash into anything.

Turned out, it was easier than everybody made it out to be.

The next thing I knew, I was pulling up in front of University Hospital.

SEVENTEEN

I RODE THE elevator up to the third floor of University Hospital, walked down to room 327. It was like any hospital room—clean, sterile, ugly, with a smell like a chemistry set. The man that I knew of as "Bob" lay in the bed. There was a tube that came out from under his sheets and went into a bag that appeared to be full of blood. There were a lot of tubes and wires attached to him. His eyes were closed, and he wasn't moving at all.

"Niles?" I said.

No motion, no flicker of eyelids, nothing.

"Niles?"

I shook his shoulder. Still nothing. His skin felt strange—kind of rubbery. I couldn't put my finger on it, but something about the feel of him gave me the creeps.

I looked around the room to see if there was anything in the room that might offer a clue as to why he was here and what he had wanted from me. I couldn't see anything.

I peeped out into the hallway, but there was nobody around, so I opened the little closet and looked inside. In the bottom lay a blue plastic bin inside of which were a pair of shoes, some folded clothes, a watch, and a cell phone. But no wallet, nothing with an ID.

That's when it hit me: a cell phone might have all kinds of information in it. Maybe even the phone number for whoever had sent him out here after me. I grabbed it, slipped it in my purse.

As I was closing the closet door, I heard a noise behind me.

It was a nurse. She must have been about six feet tall and three hundred pounds. "What are you doing in here?" she snapped.

"Sorry?"

"You heard me. What are you doing here?"

"I uh—" I tried to think of a plausible excuse. But everything I could think of had a the-cat-ate-my-home-work quality. As my eyes searched the room for some sort of answer to my predicament, my gaze settled on Niles Henry. There was a doodad attached to his finger that had a wire going up to one of those heart monitors that they always show on TV. Only this heart monitor didn't seem to be working. And the closer I looked at Niles Henry, the more it seemed like not only was he not moving—he wasn't even *breathing*.

"Isn't that machine supposed to be showing his heart rate?" I said.

"Don't think you can just change the subject, young lady," the nurse said, stepping over to the machine and flipping the ON button. Her control-top hose made a hissing sound as she walked, her huge thighs rubbing together.

The machine came on, but it was just a bunch of straight lines going across the screen.

"Oh my God," the nurse said.

"What?"

The nurse leaned over, pressed her large fingers against Niles Henry's neck. Then she looked up at me. "What did you do?"

"Me?"

"What did you do to him?"

"I didn't do anything. I just—" I squeezed my mouth shut. Telling her I was just there to rifle through his personal possessions was probably not going to help my case.

174

The nurse hit a button on the wall for the intercom. "I need a crash cart and a code team in three twenty-seven, stat!" she said.

A crash cart and a code team. I'd seen *ER* enough to know that meant Niles Henry was either dead or close to it. I started edging toward the door.

"Where are you going, young lady?"

"I'm gonna wait outside," I said.

The nurse pressed the intercom button again. "Security! Security to three twenty-seven." The big nurse made a move toward the door to stop me. But when you weigh three hundred pounds, it's hard to move real fast.

I was running down the hallway before she even got close to the door.

"Hey! Hey! You!" The nurse kept yelling at me. But once I hit the stairs, she didn't follow me.

I charged downstairs, out into the lobby, wondering how in the world I was going to get home. The answer was in the lobby. Sheriff Arnett was talking to a man in a cheap sport coat with a gold badge hanging off his belt. I was halfway across the lobby when I saw him. By then it was too late. He glanced at me in a distracted way. I almost made it to the door, but then suddenly a look of recognition crossed his face.

"Hey!" he yelled. "Come here, young lady."

I thought about bolting but didn't. It was one thing running away from a nurse. But running away from a policeman, that didn't seem smart. I stopped, tried to be calm as I said, "Hello, Sheriff."

He looked at me through narrowed eyes. "What are you doing here?"

I shrugged.

He studied me for a moment, then said, "Couple days ago, a fellow was found unconscious on the highway outside High Hopes. Looked like he'd been hit by a car. Fellow picked him up, and we called Life Flight, flew him up here to Birmingham. But this fellow, he didn't have any ID on him. No wallet, no driver's license, no nothing. Isn't that strange?"

I shrugged again, looked at the floor.

"Oh, but you wouldn't know anything about that, huh?"

Another shrug.

"This gentleman I'm speaking to, he and I are sort of coordinating our investigation into this fellow's accident." He looked at me closely. "If that's what it was."

I was about to wear out my shrugging muscles.

"You might be interested to know I was up there in his room just a few minutes ago. He didn't look real good. If he doesn't make it, this turns into a homicide investigation."

The Birmingham police investigator said to me, "So you wouldn't know who this man up there is, would you?"

I shook my head.

"See that's odd," Sheriff Arnett said. "You want to show her what you found in the pocket of John Doe's shirt?"

The investigator took out a plastic evidence bag, held it up in front of me. Inside were two photographs. The first was a crappy-looking school picture of a thirteen-year-old girl. It was me. My school picture from Clarence B. Ward Middle School in Columbus, Ohio. The second was a blurry telephoto shot of my mother walking out of the restaurant she'd been working at in Columbus.

"Why would he have this in his pocket?"

I sighed. "I wish I knew."

"Tell you what, Jim," Sheriff Arnett said. "You probably have grounds for running this gal in. But what I'm gonna do is take her back with me, have a friendly little talk on the way down to High Hopes. She's gonna tell me everything she knows."

The drive back to High Hopes seemed to take forever. I didn't say a word, and neither did Sheriff Arnett.

The sheriff rolled up in front of Ben's house, stopped. The air-conditioning was on full blast, and I was starting to get very cold.

Still the sheriff didn't speak for a while. I tried to get out, but the door lock didn't work.

"Can I just go?" I said.

As I was sitting there, his phone rang. He answered it, spoke briefly, hung up. "Well, that's it then," he said.

"What?"

"The fellow in that room just passed away."

"I told you I don't know anything about it."

"See, I'm beginning to think I underestimated this whole thing. You. Your mama. The whole thing. Y'all are in the middle of something more complicated than I gave you credit for." He paused. "I *will* get to the bottom of this."

"Kind of like you'll get to the bottom of what happened to Nancy Rydel?"

"You got no friends in this town." His voice was soft, calm. Almost a whisper. "Pretty soon you're gonna have to come crawling to me for help. And I'm just not sure whether I'm gonna give it to you or not, Chastity."

"Chass," I said. "I don't go by Chastity."

"Why does that not surprise me." He hit a button and my door lock popped up.

EIGHTEEN

THE NEXT DAY kids kept coming up to me, talking about my show on Friday night, telling me how stoked they were. Some of them seemed to think I could get fake IDs for them. I felt like some kind of celebrity. It was so weird.

At lunchtime I went outside, and Ben was standing next to the gym with Brittany and her cheerleader friends. Ben was talking, and all the girls were laughing like he was the coolest, funniest guy they had ever met.

"Hi, Ben," I said. Everybody stopped laughing.

When he saw me, Ben sort of shifted his weight a little, moving his body about two inches farther away from Brittany. They were still standing very close together, though.

"What's up?" he said. His face was kind of wooden, like he didn't really know me.

"Nothing."

The girls all stared at me blankly.

"I need to talk to you for a minute, Ben."

"What about?"

"Just come over here for a second," I said.

"Oh, she's too good for us," Melanie Reece said.

"Give her a break," Brittany said.

"Hey, I was just busting her," Melanie said. Then she turned to me and said, "So, Chass, can you hook me up with a driver's license? I'm dying to see your show tomorrow."

"I'll see what I can do," I said. Feeling a slight flush at the thought that these ice queens would actually come see *me* on Friday night instead of cruising up and down Main Street in their boyfriends' minitrucks, drinking vodka out of Coke cans. "Come on, Ben."

"See y'all soon," Ben said.

"*Soon?*" I said as we walked away. "What's up with that? Are you suddenly buds with all the cheerleaders?"

"They're not so bad," he said. "Besides, Brittany's *your* bosom buddy, not mine."

"What are you talking about?"

We had reached the parking lot. We stopped, stood there awkwardly for a minute. Ben was looking at me with this sort of dead expression on his face, like he barely noticed I was there.

"So," he said finally. "I had to find out from Brittany? From *Brittany*?"

"Find out what?"

He laughed, but it wasn't a nice laugh. "I've been your best friend—practically your *only* friend—since the minute you reached this town. And in all that time, you never bothered to tell me."

Suddenly I understood what he was talking about. The other day when we were driving around together, I had told Brittany the whole story about my life on the run with Mom. She must have told him.

"Chass Pureheart isn't even your *real name?*" he said. "You and your mom are some kind of fugitives or something? Traveling around changing your names and stuff?" He shook his head, disgusted. "I thought I knew you, but I guess I was wrong. I never knew you at all."

"I'm sorry, Ben!" I said. "It's not you. It's—I've never told anybody in my life. Never."

"Except your best friend Brittany."

"It just slipped out . . ." I put my head down, stared at the ground. "I wanted to tell you. I've wanted to tell you for so long. I just—"

"Whatever." His voice was cold, his eyes dead.

"Ben, please . . ."

"So what was it you wanted?" he said sharply.

I hesitated for a second. Ben was looking at me without moving at all. He'd had a lot of homework and had barely spoken to me the night before, so I still hadn't told him about Niles Henry. "That guy?" I said finally. "The one you hit with the Batmobile?"

Ben just kept looking at me.

"He's dead."

Ben took a step back, like I'd kicked him in the face. But for a minute he didn't say anything. I was going to tell him about Sheriff Arnett being there, about how suspicious it seemed to me that the guy had died just about the same time that he was visited by the sheriff. But suddenly I felt like I had forgotten how to talk.

"Who *are* you?" Ben said finally. Then he turned silently away from me and began walking back toward the building.

I was about to follow him when I saw the assistant principal, Mr. Winbush, stalking across the yard directly toward me. As usual, his face was red with anger.

Before I could move, Mr. Winbush grabbed me by the arm. "Come with me, young lady!" he said.

Two minutes later I was sitting in his office while he stood over me, jabbing his finger in my face.

"Where were you yesterday afternoon?" he shouted. The Bush never talked at a normal volume.

"Oh, gosh, Mr. Winbush, I totally forgot about detention hall." I tried to look all innocent.

"Don't give me that look!" he shouted. "I understand you cut school yesterday too!"

"I don't know if you heard about my mom . . ." I said, trying to sound pitiful. I hated using my mom as an excuse. But what else was I going to do?

"Normally, Chastity, I would be sympathetic. But it seems like you've taken advantage of her absence to get in all kind of trouble." He reached into a desk drawer, pulled out a paper sack, dumped its contents on the worn but spotless top of his fake wood desk. "You want to tell me about this?"

It was a pile of ID cards.

I looked at them expressionlessly.

"Fake IDs. I got a little tip and seized thirty-seven fake ID cards from your good buddy Jay-Jay Brice."

"Jay-Jay! I barely even know the guy."

"Well, apparently you have some little musical performance you're planning to do at some nightclub around here? Does that ring a bell? And all the kids are trying to get fake IDs so they can come."

I couldn't believe that lots of people actually wanted to come. Much less that they'd go to the trouble of buying fake IDs so they could do it. "Really?"

"Like you didn't know." He laughed his loud, bitter laugh.

"I'm serious. I have no idea what you're talking about."

He glared at me. "Just for lying to me, that's another week of detention hall."

"Yes, sir."

"Get back to class."

After school was out, I walked down to the auditorium, where they had detention hall, looked in the back door, and saw all the kids lolling around, looking bored. Coach Boorman sat up front wearing his too-tight pants, his feet on the desk, flirting with a couple of the dumb girls from the voc-ed program.

I walked down front and said, "Hey, Coach," in my flirtiest voice.

"What?"

"Can I ask a favor? I have something I *so* need to do this afternoon. Can you mark me present for detention hall?"

He blinked, looked at me for a minute.

I leaned over like I had with the guy that owned that bar, Ronnie's, giving him a little peep down the neck of my shirt. Kind of as an experiment. Coach Boorman's gaze dropped from my face.

"Come on!" I felt mad for some reason, but I squeezed the anger out of my mouth, making it sweet as pancake syrup. I leaned down a little farther. "Pretty please with sugar on top?"

He tilted his head toward the door. "A'ight. Go on." I started walking. "Hey! Girl! If the Bush catches you, I'm gonna erase that little check mark in the roll book."

I giggled like I thought he was the wittiest guy I'd ever met. "Yes, sir," I said. Brittany would have been proud of me I'm sure.

I walked out to the parking lot in time to find Ben and Brittany talking. He was saying something, and then she was laughing and putting her hand on his arm.

"Hey, Chass!" she said when she saw me. "You blowing off detention hall?"

"Yeah."

"So what happened yesterday at the hospital?"

I told her and Ben all about the visit to the hospital, about how Niles was dead when I got there. Then I pulled out the phone I'd stolen from Niles Henry's belongings. "Check this out," I said. "I've got his phone."

"Whose phone?"

"Bob. Niles Henry. Whatever his name is."

"Chass, you are crazy, girl!" Brittany said. "What are you gonna do with it?"

"We know he works for this private investigator, Edward Wong. But who does Wong work for? Maybe Niles Henry's got the number programmed into his phone."

"Here." Ben took the phone from me, started punching buttons. "There's not much battery left."

"Check and see if it has a list of the most recent calls."

"What do you think I'm doing?" He scowled, irritated. "Oh crap. It ran out of juice."

"What kind of phone is it?" I said. "Maybe we can find somebody to recharge it."

"It's a Samsung."

"Brandi Chun has a Samsung," Brittany said. "Let me call her."

Brittany got on her phone, made a call, got hold of Brandi Chun.

"Tell her to meet us at the library downtown," I said.

"The *library*? Why?"

"I've got an idea," I said.

"I'll go get her, then y'all can meet us there," Brittany said. Then she walked across the parking lot, leaving me standing with Ben.

Ben was just kind of looking at me like he barely knew me.

"Ben," I said, "how many times do I have to apologize? I'm sorry I didn't tell you about me and Mom. But it's complicated."

He shrugged.

"Please don't be mad at me."

"Mad?" He gave me a big empty smile. "I'm not mad."

We drove to the library. Brandi and Tiffany were waiting outside for us. Fortunately Brandi's charger fit Niles Henry's phone, so we got it charging. Then I went over to the computer, logged on to the Internet, and did a Web search of the names on the ID cards Mom had ordered from Dwayne Crooks.

They were all corporate ID cards. The names on the cards didn't raise any hits, but the companies all had something in common. They were all subsidiaries of Apex Global Media. One was for a location in Torrance, California, and the other two were located in Atlanta.

"Apex again," I said.

Ben was looking over my shoulder. "What's Apex?"

"My mom's been doing something for years, something to do with this company Apex Global Media. She has all these fake corporate ID cards. But I don't have any idea what she was after."

"Why Apex?" Brittany said.

I shook my head. "Let's check out the phone again," I said.

I picked it up, switched it on, thumbed through the menus until I found a list of the most recently called phone numbers. I recognized most of the recent calls as having gone to EW Investigations. But the very last call he made was to another number, a number that was listed on his calling list as MR. SMITH. Somehow I had a hunch that whoever was on the other end of that line was not named Smith.

I dialed the number nervously. After two rings, a man answered. His voice was quiet but somehow radiated authority. "I specifically instructed you not to call this number," he said.

I handed the phone to Ben. "Say, 'Who am I speaking to?'" I whispered.

"Who am I speaking to?" Ben said tentatively. He frowned then handed the phone back to me. "They hung up on me," he said.

"I guess he saw on caller ID who it was," I said. "And he didn't want to talk to Niles."

"What if we called from another number?" Brittany said. "I could do my sheriff's investigator number again."

"Worth a try," I said.

She took out her phone, dialed the number off the display on Niles Henry's phone.

"Hello, sir," she said. "This is Sheriff's Investigator Arnett from Yallee County, Alabama. Who am I speaking to?" She listened for a moment. "Yes, sir, that was my partner who just called you. We're investigating the, uh, the disappearance of a John Doe here in Yallee County. We found his phone and we're calling everybody on his calling list to determine who he is. Sir, don't pretend you don't know who this person is. In so many words you just told my partner that you knew who was calling me. Sir . . . sir . . . now don't try and dodge my question. I have your number, so I *will* find out who you are. You might as well save me the time." She winked at me. It was amazing how she managed to make herself sound older, more serious, like a real cop. I felt envious for a minute. "Uh-huh. So who is the gentleman who owns this phone? And what relationship is he to you? I see. So is he here working for you or not? Uh-huh. Uh-huh. So then why would he be calling you? I see. I see. Thank you for your help, sir."

She thumbed the OFF button with her bright red fingernail.

"So what did he say?" '

"He said that Niles Henry was a private investigator that he hired a few months ago. He said that he fired Niles for incompetence, and that now Niles was bugging him because he refused to pay."

"So I assume he said that he didn't know why Niles was here in Alabama?"

Brittany nodded. "Right." She smiled. "But he was lying."

"How do you know?" Ben said.

She showed off her teeth. "My dad's a cop, Ben. I can tell when people are lying. It's in my blood."

"Yeah, but what's his name?" I said.

"Shoot. I knew you were gonna ask that." Brittany wrinkled her nose. "Carl Something. It was Dutch-sounding. Or German? Van Something? Von Something?"

I looked at Ben. "Not Kyle Van Epps?"

Brittany grinned. "Kyle Van Epps! That's it!"

Brittany looked at me then at Ben then at me again. "Who's Kyle Van Epps?"

"He's only the president of one of the largest media companies in the world," I said.

"Apex," she said.

"Apex."

As we were standing there looking at the little phone in Brittany's hand, I heard a voice behind me.

"Hi, Chass." A man's voice, cheery sounding.

I turned, and there was a tall Asian guy in a long black leather coat. Edward Wong.

"Everybody," I said softly, "you need to get out of here right now."

I started backing away from the private investigator. "Chass," he said, "hold on. Calm down. I just want to talk."

Edward Wong turned slightly so that I could see under his coat. He had a gun clipped to his belt. My eyes met Ben's. I could see that Ben saw the gun too.

"You guys aren't part of this," I said to the other kids. "Just walk away, let me handle this."

I don't know what got into Ben, but instead of walking away, he picked up a book and threw it at Edward Wong. It sailed past Wong's head.

At that same moment Brittany started screaming at the top of her lungs.

Ben hurled himself at Wong. Wong sidestepped so smoothly that it seemed like he barely moved. But the next thing I knew, Ben was flying through the air and smashing headfirst into a table.

Edward Wong looked around, saw the faces staring at him from all over the library. He turned toward me, smiled. "We'll talk again soon, Chass," he said softly.

Then he turned and walked briskly out the front door of the library.

Brittany stopped screaming, ran over to Ben. Ben looked up at her, and there was blood all over his face. He had a cut over his eye.

"God, Ben," she said. "That was so brave."

"Are you okay, Ben?" I said. I put my hand on his face, trying to wipe away the blood. He pushed my hand away.

"I'm fine," he mumbled. "I'm fine."

Brittany helped him to his feet. "We're gonna go now, Chass," she said. "It's time to tell Dad."

She put her arm around Ben's waist, supporting him. He looked slightly dazed. They started walking toward the exit.

"Wait, no!" I called after her. "Brittany, don't!"

"She's right, Chass," Ben said. "This is out of control."

"*You're* out of control, Chass," Brittany said. "You almost got Ben killed just now."

"Me? Ben's the one who . . ."

I stood there watching them as they disappeared out the door, feeling like the bottom had dropped out of my stomach.

NINETEEN

I HAD TO walk all the way out to Ben's house, two or three miles from downtown. It was starting to get dark when I got there. The sheriff's Cadillac was sitting at the end of the long dirt driveway.

I walked in the front door, and there was Ben and his mother and father and Sheriff Arnett sitting in the living room, waiting for me.

Before I even had a chance to say hello, Ben's mom was yelling at me. "Chass, what were you thinking!"

Ben's dad put his hand on her arm. "Tina, don't."

She jerked her hand away from him. "We extended our hospitality, our home, our love to you, Chass! And how did you return our kindness? You nearly got our son killed!"

"Tina, I'll handle this," Sheriff Arnett said firmly.

Ben's mom glared at me, then stood and stalked out of the room.

"Chastity," the sheriff said. "We're all a little upset here. I think that's understandable don't you?"

I slumped down in a chair, put my hands in my pockets, looked at the floor.

"You've put my daughter and their son in a lot of danger."

I shrugged.

"Look at me when I'm talking, young lady."

I looked at him. His blue eyes were cold and unsympathetic.

"Let's hear it," he said. "I want to know everything that's happened. I want to know what your mother was into. I want to know every single scrap of information you have. And I want it now."

"I'll tell you everything I know," I said. "But first . . ."

"First what?"

I took a deep breath, sat up as straight as I could. "But first, you have to tell me what happened to Nancy Rydel."

The sheriff looked at me for a long time. "You're in no position to bargain."

"Oh for godsake," Mr. Purvis said. "Let's just get it over with, Doyle. We've been covering it up for—"

"Shut up, Addison," the sheriff snapped at him. Then he turned to me. "Up. Get up, little girl."

I didn't move, just shoved my hands deeper in my pockets.

"All right then," he said mildly. Then he pulled a pair of handcuffs off his belt, walked quickly across the room, yanked me to my feet, and spun me around. Seconds later I felt the bite of steel on my wrists. "Let's go," he said.

"Come on, Doyle," Addison said. "This is unnecessary."

"I said shut up," the sheriff said. "Let's go, Chastity."

I looked at Ben. "Ben . . . ," I said.

Ben just looked away.

The sheriff shoved me toward the door.

Ten minutes later I was sitting in a small green-painted room in the back of the sheriff's office. The room smelled like cigarettes and had a big mirror on one wall. My hands were cuffed to a big shiny steel ring on the edge of a steel table. I was alone.

I kept thinking, *What would Mom do? What would Mom do?*

I must have sat there for an hour—maybe even two—before the sheriff finally came back into the room. I had no way of knowing what time it was. I still hadn't eaten supper. The sheriff was followed by a large black woman. I recognized her as Mrs. Oglesby, the lady from the Department of Human Resources. She still had a look on her face like I was giving off some kind of stink.

"You remember Mrs. Oglesby from DHR?" Sheriff Arnett smiled blandly at me. "I'll let y'all talk."

He went back out, closed the door behind him.

"You are in a great, great, great deal of trouble, Chastity," she said.

I just looked at the wall.

"I do *not* appreciate being dragged out of my home when I'm putting my children to bed, young lady," she said.

"I didn't ask for you to come here," I said.

"Nonetheless, here I am."

"What's going to happen now?" I said.

"The sheriff has requested that I be here to act in loco parentis, while he interrogates you."

"In loco what?"

"Parentis. That's the legal term for a person who is designated as a guardian. The law requires a parent or guardian be present when a juvenile is questioned by a member of law enforcement."

"Okay. And after I'm questioned?"

"I'll transport you to the juvenile diversion facility at Tuscaloosa."

"So you're saying I'm going to jail."

"The juvenile diversion facility is not a jail."

"Do they lock the doors at night?"

Mrs. Oglesby looked at me with her disapproving eyes and didn't answer.

I wanted my mom so bad. I wanted to just cry and cry and have her hold me and tell me everything was going to be okay and the world would be normal again. But I knew that wasn't in the cards. So I had to be strong. This woman was not on my side. Not even vaguely. "Bring in the sheriff," I said.

Mrs. Oglesby rose in her cloud of dignity, slapped her palm on the door with her long yellow fingernails splayed out in the air.

Sheriff Arnett came in and sat down. "All right," he said. "Are you ready to talk?"

"I didn't ask this woman to be here," I said. "I want a lawyer."

The sheriff crossed his arms. "As long as a legal guardian is present, the law does not require—"

"She is not my legal guardian," I said. "Show me a piece of paper that proves she's my legal guardian."

The sheriff took out a stick of gum, popped it in

his mouth. "You think you're awful smart don't you, Chastity."

"Would you people stop calling me Chastity!" I yelled. "I go by Chass. Chass. *C-H-A-S-S*. Is that so hard?"

The room was silent.

"Show me a paper proving she's my guardian or get me a lawyer."

"Wait here," the sheriff said. He got up and walked out of the room.

Mrs. Oglesby looked at her watch, then got out an emery board and started fooling with her nails. She didn't look at me once.

After a while the door opened, and a man in a suit came into the room.

"Hi, Chastity," he said. "My name is David Leung. I'm an attorney from Birmingham. I'm here to represent you."

My heart began to pound. The lawyer—if that's what he was—who was smiling genially at me was a tall well-dressed Asian guy.

Edward Wong.

I sunk as deep into my chair as I could. "I don't want this lawyer," I said desperately.

"Mrs. Oglesby," Edward Wong said to the social worker, "I have tried to ascertain your status here, and it seems that your status as guardian is, at best, ambiguous.

That said, the rights of my client would best be protected if you would step outside."

"Don't leave me alone with him," I said.

Edward Wong smiled genially. "I'm here to protect you," he said. "You have nothing to worry about."

"Please," I said.

"Don't look at me for help," Mrs. Oglesby said. "You wanted a lawyer, little girl—now you got one." Then she walked out the door. It clanged ominously shut.

"You have been arrested on charges of breaking and entering, criminal mischief, vandalism, obstruction, tampering with evidence, a couple other things," Edward Wong said. He smiled pleasantly.

I looked at him blankly.

"Which means that, unless they decide otherwise, they'll send you to the juvenile home up in Tuscaloosa until next Tuesday, when you go before a judge and are formally charged. In a criminal trial that would be called arraignment. In juvenile court it's called . . . well, since I don't practice law in Alabama, I have no idea what it's called. But whatever the case, they'll probably set bail at that point, and if you have the money, you can go free. Otherwise you will be in the clutches of the juvenile justice system for the foreseeable future."

"I could scream," I said.

"The room's soundproofed. I could bash your face

in before they ever heard you. But, hey, that's not why I'm here."

"Are you really a lawyer?" I said.

He smiled. "I have a little ID card that says I am."

"But you're not really a lawyer."

Edward Wong kept smiling. He had a very bright smile, like a Hong Kong action movie star. "I carry all kinds of little ID cards in the glove compartment of my truck. Sometimes it comes in handy for a private investigator to pretend to be something he's not. Insurance adjuster, doctor, massage therapist . . . lawyer."

"How did you even know I was here?"

"I was watching you from the road near your little buddy Ben's house. I saw the sheriff put you into his car. You were wearing cuffs. Being the genius of deductive reasoning that I am, I figured that he was bringing you here. And that you would need a lawyer."

"Oh."

"So, I just came right over, presented my bar card, and told them I represented you."

We sat for a minute without saying anything. I was trying to figure out what to do. I could hear the air conditioner humming, but otherwise I couldn't hear a thing. He was right about the room being soundproofed.

He was still smiling as he said, "So where is it, Chastity?"

I sighed loudly. "Not again."

His smile faded. "I've been on the trail of this thing for as long as you've been alive. You better believe I'm not about to quit today. Now start talking."

"Your boy Niles Henry asked me the same thing. He said he was going to kill me if I didn't tell him. I didn't tell him either. You want to guess why?"

Edward Wong shrugged.

"Because I don't have a freakin' clue what it is that you want."

"The tape."

"The tape!" I said sarcastically. "Well, now we're getting somewhere. Niles never even told me that much. He just told me to dig my grave, and then he was like, 'Where is it? Where is it? Where is it?' Where is *what*? He never bothered to tell me."

Wong's eyes narrowed a little. "Tell me exactly what happened to him."

I told him the story of how "Bob" picked me up and threatened to kill me, how Ben hit him with the Batmobile.

Edward Wong shook his head sadly. "I'm sure he didn't intend to kill you. He's just a kind of theatrical guy."

"And I suppose you didn't kill Dwayne Crooks either."

"Who?"

"The fake-ID guy up in Birmingham."

"Oh. That guy." He laughed. "Matter of fact, no, I didn't kill him. Shot a couple holes in his ceiling though. He suddenly got very helpful after that." Edward Wong laughed. "In fact, he even made me an Alabama Bar Association card. On very short notice. For free. Out of the generosity of his heart. Isn't that cool?"

"So you want a tape. A tape of what?"

Edward Wong stared at me for a long time. "Where's your mom?" he said finally.

I had a sudden flash of hope. If this guy didn't know where she was, then he obviously hadn't killed her. I decided to pretend I knew more than I did. "Wouldn't you like to know," I said.

"Look, Chass, I can get you out of here. But I need a little cooperation in return."

I looked at him for a long time, trying to figure out what his angle was. I really had no idea. "What do you mean *get me out*?" I said.

He leaned forward, dropped his voice. "Listen carefully . . ."

TWENTY

EDWARD WONG BANGED on the door with his fist. After a minute, Sheriff Arnett answered the door.

"My client needs to use the bathroom."

The sheriff came in, unlocked the cuffs that bound my wrists to the steel ring on the table. "Let's go," he said.

I stood and followed him out the door and down the hallway. He pointed to a bathroom door. "I'll wait out here," he said.

I went inside, turned on the water, and waited. After

about a minute I heard somebody yell, "Help me! Please! Help!"

It sounded like Edward Wong's voice.

I counted to ten, then poked my head out the door. The sheriff was gone, and the hallway was empty.

I trotted down the hallway, turned left, and ducked into a broom closet. After about a minute someone knocked gently on the door. I went out, and there was Edward Wong. "Quick! Quick!" he said.

We walked toward an emergency exit. Edward Wong pushed on the door. It didn't open.

"Uh-oh," he said. "There must be some kind of emergency override."

"What's that mean?"

"Doesn't matter. Follow me."

We turned and walked quickly back up the hallway, turned toward the front entrance to the sheriff's office. A deputy was sitting at the front counter, feet up on the table, reading a magazine about guns.

Edward Wong smiled easily at him. "Can you buzz me and my client out, bud?" he said.

The deputy looked at Wong, looked at me, then back at Wong.

"Where's *she* going?"

"Released on her own recognizance."

The deputy squinted suspiciously at Wong. "I better check with the sheriff."

"What you think I'm staging, a jail break here, pal? They'd take away my law license in a heartbeat if I did something like that."

The deputy scratched his head. "Yeah, I reckon you right."

He reached over, hit a red button. The door buzzed, and Edward Wong said, "After you, darling."

I walked out the door.

Somewhere behind me I heard someone yelling, "Where'd she go? Where's that lawyer?" It sounded like the sheriff's voice.

"Nice and easy, nice and easy," Edward Wong said. We were in the lobby now. "We're walking, we're walking, we're acting natural."

I did like he said, walking out the front door of the building.

"I think this is the part where you and me start running," Edward Wong said.

We both ran across the road to where his black SUV was parked.

"Get in," he said.

"Are you crazy?" I said.

"Unless you want to spend the rest of your life in

some juvenile home," he said, "you better get in the car."

I got in the car, slammed the door.

Across the street deputies came pouring out of the front door of the sheriff's office, followed by the sheriff himself.

"Don't move," Wong said. "This car has heavily tinted windows. But if you move, they might catch the motion inside."

I sat there frozen, my hands trembling. Sheriff's deputies ran across the street, waving flashlights in the dark and looking around all the cars.

"Don't move," Wong whispered tensely. "Do. Not. Move."

I didn't.

Sheriff Arnett walked across the street, looking angrily up and down the road. Finally he approached the SUV where we were sitting, stared at it for a long time, then came over and looked underneath, as though expecting me to be hiding under it. He couldn't have been more than three feet from me. He stood up, stared at the window where I was sitting. It seemed like he was looking right into my eyes. But I guess he couldn't see anything.

After a moment he turned, walked back across the street, yelling orders at his men.

"Good girl," Edward Wong said softly. "Gooooood girl." It sounded like he was talking to his favorite puppy.

"I'm not a dog," I said.

He looked over at me, studied my face for a moment. "I had noticed that," he said. "Actually."

Five minutes later, the street was clear.

"All right," Edward Wong said. "We need to get you into a hotel somewhere. Maybe Birmingham. Maybe even Atlanta. It's possible that you're in a lot of danger right now."

"It's *possible*!" I said.

"Look, I don't know who you think I am but—"

"I think you're a private investigator working for Kyle Van Epps," I said.

He looked at me and blinked. Then he started to laugh. "Me? Working for Van Epps? What in the world made you think that?"

"I managed to get hold of your boy Niles Henry's cell phone. He had Kyle Van Epps on his speed dial."

Wong stared at me for a moment. Then his face got hard. "Son of a—"

"What?"

Wong shook his head. "Nothing," he said. "But I promise you I'm not working for Van Epps."

I didn't believe him. "So if you're not working for Kyle Van Epps," I said, "then what *are* you doing here?"

"Working on unfinished business," he said.

"You're going to have to do better than that," I said.

"You're going to have to trust me," he said.

"Trust *you*? Give me one good reason why."

He didn't say anything. I took advantage of the break in his concentration to pop the door lock and open the door.

"Chass, wait! I just got you out of jail."

"Yeah, and you just bashed my friend's face to a pulp too," I said. "See you around."

"Well, if he hadn't attacked me, I wouldn't have had to do that."

I slammed the door.

He rolled down the window. "I can help you!" he called.

I turned around. "How? Do you know where my mom is? Do you even know if she's alive?"

He hesitated.

"Yeah," I said. "I thought not."

It took me a long time to hike out to Ben's house. It was close to eleven when I got there.

I went up and knocked on the door. Ben's dad answered in his bathrobe. "Doyle said you'd be held at the station all night. How did you get out?"

"I kind of escaped," I said. "Could we talk?"

"You *escaped*!" Mrs. Purvis was coming out of the bedroom "Don't let her in this house, Addison. I will not have an escaped prisoner in my home. In the past three days she has succeeded in almost getting Ben arrested, getting his face smashed by some criminal with a gun and—"

Mr. Purvis said, "Honey . . ."

"Forget it. Just forget it!" She waved her hands angrily. "You're not even listening to me."

Mrs. Purvis had always been so nice to me. Now that she had suddenly turned on me, I felt sick.

"Can we go out to your studio then, Mr. Purvis?" I said. "I just want to talk."

Ben's father looked at me for a long time. "Yeah," he said finally. "I guess we could do that."

Ben came out of his room, looked at me quizzically. "What's going on?"

"Nothing, Ben!" Mrs. Purvis said. "Go back in your room!"

"Enough!" Mr. Purvis shouted. I had never seen him lose his temper before, never even heard him raise his voice. "Tina, please, just butt out, okay?"

Mrs. Purvis stared at him like he'd just slapped her. "So now she's got *you* under her spell too?"

"Please. I'm sorry." Mr. Purvis's voice dropped. "Please, honey, I have to do this."

"Whatever." Ben's mother slammed the door.

"You too, Ben," Mr. Purvis said softly. Then turning to me: "Come on, Chass."

I followed him through the house, out the back door, and into his gloomy studio. He opened the big bay door and stood leaning against the doorframe, staring out at the night.

"What happened to Nancy Rydel?" I said finally.

He didn't answer for a long time. The night had gone inky black now, and the stars were very clear in the sky. There was no moon. But I could see something gleaming on Ben's father's face. He didn't speak again for a long time. It might have been ten minutes. But I knew somehow that eventually he'd keep talking. Whatever had happened, it had been bottled up in there for too long.

"My mother died when I was about ten," Addison Purvis said finally. "After she died, Daddy kind of lost it. He'd always liked taking a drink. But it got pretty bad. He'd go up to Birmingham or Tuscaloosa, come back with some college girl. She'd stay with him for a night or two and then be gone. I didn't really understand it at the time. But then I got older, and I started getting the picture. I got real mad at my father. Poor bastard. I realize now that he was sad. He was lonely. He was lost, I guess, without Mama."

He laughed sadly.

"Anyway, one day when I was in high school I came home, and there was Nancy Rydel sitting at our dinner table eating a sandwich. I was about to ask her what she was doing there. But I didn't really need to. I already knew. She was like the school slut, you know. Can you imagine how that feels? Your own dad hanging out with the school slut? It was pathetic. It was disgusting. I just walked out of the house.

"We had a football game that night. I went to the game, and I was so mad, I just took out all my anger on the other team. It was me and Jimmy Laws and Doyle Arnett that did all the scoring. And we just . . . I mean we *killed* that other team. I got in a fight at the end, though, knocked this guy down, got thrown out of the game. We had a perfect record that year, and that was the final game of the regular season. So me and Jimmy and Doyle went out to celebrate. I was such a choirboy—I never drank or anything. But I was so mad still that when Jimmy said why don't we go buy some moonshine from this old redneck outside town, I said okay.

"We ended up back at my house. And there's Nancy Rydel still there. My dad's in the bedroom, and Nancy's out in the living room with her clothes half off, watching TV. And I just looked at her and said, 'What are you doing here?'

"She said, 'Watching TV.'

"I said, 'No, you're banging my dad.'

"Well, she just laughed. And I said, 'We just won the big game. We're conquering heroes. We all deserve a reward.'

"She just laughed again. So I said, 'Either you give me and my buddies a reward or you can get the hell out of my house.'

"My dad came out and said, 'Leave her alone, Addison.'

"So I looked over at my dad, and then I just punched her in the face. Wham! She fell down on the couch and didn't move. I mean I really wanted to punch my dad. It was *him* I was mad at. Not her. She was just this poor sad little creature that wanted some affection and had figured out that boys would be nice to her if she . . . you know . . ."

He sighed. "Well, my dad starts yelling at me. And I said, 'You gonna do something about it, old man?' My dad was a lot shorter than me, and he'd had too much to drink, and he just looked at me, and he knew he was overmatched." Ben's dad put his hands over his face. "I can still see the look on Daddy's face. He was so sad and so defeated. You know, he knew exactly why I'd hit that girl, and he must have just felt like the worst, weakest, most pitiful man in the world. Man, it just wrecked him.

"So I shoved Nancy Rydel over, and I sat down on

the couch and started watching TV. After a minute Nancy regained consciousness, and she got up and started carrying on and crying. Eventually we got her calmed down, and then she went out onto the back porch with my dad.

"Long story short, Jimmy and Doyle and I polished off the moonshine, and eventually I kind of blacked out. About two o'clock in the morning, somebody woke me up. It was Doyle Arnett. He said, 'You better come here.' So I stumbled out, and there's Nancy Rydel lying in the middle of the floor on the porch.

"I said, 'Let her sleep.'

"Doyle went, 'Man, she's not sleeping.'

"I reached down, rolled her over, and her face was just *all* smashed up. I mean I hit her once, but nothing like that." He took a long shuddering breath. "She was dead."

Ben's father kept staring out at the black horizon.

"And then I looked at my hands. My knuckles were all skinned up. There was blood on them. And honestly to this day I don't know if it was from getting in the fight during the game. Or if it was from . . . something else. I don't remember anything about that night."

"So Doyle looked at my hands, and he said, 'You know we can't tell Daddy about this.' His father was the sheriff back then. I went, 'We have to.' And I heard a voice behind me. It was Jimmy. He said, 'Doyle's right. Does anybody know she was here?' I said I didn't know.

"Jimmy said, 'Get her ankles.' He grabbed her under her arms. I went, 'No. I'm calling your dad, Doyle.' But Doyle just grabbed her ankles, and they dragged her down the stairs. I sat there in the kitchen, crying like a baby. Eventually they came back up the stairs, and Jimmy went, 'It's done, Addison. Shut up and quit crying. When she comes up missing, we don't know anything.'"

Ben's father slumped down and sat on the ground. "Within a couple of days, everybody started looking for her. And apparently her father knew that she had come over to our house, because he started making accusations. But there was no way to prove it, so nothing ever came of it. Around Christmas, Jimmy skipped town. And after that, the whole thing died.

"So one day when I got home Daddy came up out of the basement. He was all dirty and sweaty, and he said, 'I put a new wall in down there. Just in case.'

"And I said to him, 'How did you know?'

"He said, 'I'm not a fool, you know. It's my fault, and I recognize that. But I'm not a fool.' Then he went, 'I think it would be best if when you left for college, you didn't come back here again.'

"And I said, 'Yeah, probably so.' And he didn't take a drink or look at another woman the rest of that year. And he was really sweet to me. Paid attention to me in ways that he hadn't done in years. It was strange. But then

I graduated, and I got on the Greyhound bus, and I left town. And I didn't come back until the old man died."

I nodded. "So why is it that you and Sheriff Arnett don't get along?" I said.

"I don't even know. Things soured between us after that night; I guess we just learned some things about each other that night. Things we didn't like. And once something goes sour with somebody like that, you can't ever bring it back. Eventually we got in a fight over a girl, and I beat the crap out of him. It was just dumb kid stuff. But it was kind of the icing on the cake."

"So you killed her?" I said.

He shook his head. "Did I? I really don't remember. Mad as I was at her and at my father, I just don't feel like I'm the kind of person that would do a thing like that." He took a deep, ragged breath. "But I don't know for sure. Maybe anybody is capable of killing somebody under the right circumstances."

I thought about it for a while. Finally I said, "Did my mother ever ask you about Nancy Rydel?"

He turned and looked at me with a puzzled expression barely discernible in the dark. "Why would she? Nobody knew about that night. Nobody except me and Doyle and Jimmy."

"Huh," I said.

"Why would you ask that?"

"She went to that old house for a reason. She had started breaking down that wall in the basement. It's the last thing she did before she disappeared."

Mr. Purvis stared at me. "That doesn't make sense."

"I think Sheriff Arnett moved the body."

Mr. Purvis laughed hollowly. "No. *I* moved the body. *I* chased you out of the house." He paused, frowned. "Ben didn't tell you that?" He kept looking at me. "Ben saw me clear as a bell. He threw that shovel at me, and then he saw it was me. He didn't tell you that?"

I shook my head.

Mr. Purvis sighed a long, wracking sigh. "Oh, that poor kid. I'm letting him down, just like my old man did me."

We sat there for a while, and Mr. Purvis stared into the night.

Finally he stood up. He had a funny look in his eyes. "I'm going to go see Doyle in the morning. I'll explain some things to him and I'll . . . I'll take whatever I've got coming."

I didn't say anything.

"While I'm at it, I'll square things between you and him. I don't want them carting you off to the juvenile home tomorrow."

"He won't go for it. He's got it in for me."

"Doyle's not that tough. He comes on strong, but when you push him hard, he backs down."

"If you say so."

"Go back inside and go to sleep."

"I don't think your wife will let me," I said.

"She's like a mother bear. She's protecting her little cub. When she understands what's been going on here, she'll be okay with you. She loves you almost like a daughter, Chass. I promise you she does."

We walked back into the house. Ben's Mom was sitting at the dinner table, wearing a robe, her hair pulled back in a ponytail.

"I want her out right now," she said, not meeting my eye.

"Tina."

"I'm not debating this. I will not have an escaped prisoner in my house. I don't care if you take her to a hotel, take her to jail, take her to her apartment—just get her out of here. She's caused enough trouble under this roof."

"You ain't seen nothing yet," Ben's dad said.

"What does *that* mean, Addison?"

Ben's father just shook his head and then turned to me. "I'm sorry, Chass," he said. "Can you stay at your apartment by yourself tonight?"

I nodded, trying to blink back the tears.

"All right," he said. "Grab your things. I'll give you a ride."

TWENTY-ONE

AS I WALKED up to my apartment, I picked up the newspapers that were scattered by the door and went inside. It was the first time I'd been in our apartment in about a week. It smelled funny—stale, foreign. It didn't seem like a home at all. More like a cheap hotel. No art or family photos on the walls, secondhand furniture, no books or CDs on the shelves. I knew I wouldn't be able to sleep. After a while I picked up today's paper and flipped to the classifieds, not really expecting to find anything.

But amazingly—there it was:

ROOM FOR RENT. CHILDREN, YES. PETS, YES.
SMOKERS, NO.

I blinked. I couldn't believe it. Mom was alive! I had
to start over and read it again.

ROOM FOR RENT. CHILDREN, YES. PETS, YES.
SMOKERS, NO. LOUD MUSIC, NO. 223 SQUARE
FEET. CALL MRS. MAIN ON WEDNESDAYS
ANYTIME AFTER MIDNIGHT. IF I'M NOT HOME,
COME IN AND LOOK AROUND. THE KEY IS IN
THE MAILBOX.

I looked at the clock. It was 11:57. A bolt of electricity ran through me. Mom was going to be at 223 Main
Street in three minutes. I had no car, and Main Street was
probably a mile away. My heart started slamming wildly
in my chest.

I burst out the door and started running.

Let me just say this. I am not a jock. When they did
the presidential physical fitness thing and all that stuff? I
was always like the last girl across the finish line in the
mile run. I mean I'm not fat or anything, but I just don't
seem to have much wind. Or maybe I just don't care.

Whatever the case, my point is that covering long distances on foot in short amounts of time is not my thing.

I tried to settle into a rhythm, but I couldn't do it. My shoes were biting into my feet and my lungs felt like they were full of razor blades. I looked at my watch. Four minutes. I just couldn't run any more. I started walking, walking as fast as I could.

A car drove by me, slowed, then speeded up. I couldn't see inside the windows. My stomach jumped. Could that be Mom?

I looked at my watch. One minute.

I broke into a run again. Fire tore up the left side of my chest. Something was squishing inside my shoe. Like maybe I was bleeding.

I was six minutes late. I arrived in front of 223 Main Street so out of breath I could hardly stand up. I looked around. Nobody.

The building numbered 223 turned out to be a bank—Planters and Southern Bank, the biggest bank in town. I looked up and down the street. Nothing moved.

You have to understand, downtown High Hopes is not like downtown New York City or something. It's one of those roll-up-the-sidewalk-at-sundown places. Come five-thirty, six o'clock, the downtown area is a ghost town. By nine o'clock it's like the set of one of these creepy movies where somebody wakes up and everybody in the world has mysteriously disappeared. You practically expected zombies to start stumbling down the street toward you. It's *that* dead.

So it's not like I would have missed my mom if she was there.

There were no cars on the street. Nobody parked in front of the courthouse. No lights on in the windows of buildings nearby. I suppose they had a dispatcher down at the sheriff's office. But you wouldn't have known it from looking.

Six minutes late. Mom just wasn't there.

I bent over one of the scraggly bushes and thought for a minute I was going to puke. Not because I was so angry at myself. I had just run too far, too fast. And still, I was six minutes late. What if she'd come and gone? Maybe it was too dangerous for her to stay.

And now I'd missed her.

Or maybe she was just late.

I waited until a few minutes past one o'clock. But she never came.

Somewhere along the way I pulled out the ad from the paper and read it over again.

If I'm not home, come in and look around. The key is in the mailbox.

What did that mean? It wasn't part of the message that we'd agreed on.

I noticed the bank I was standing in front of had a big black mailbox. I opened it up. There was nothing inside. I walked up and down the road, checking the mailboxes of all the nearby stores—the ones that had mailboxes anyhow—but I found nothing. No keys, no letters, nothing at all.

I went back to the apartment, lay down and stared at the ceiling until the sky started turning light again.

TWENTY-TWO

FRIDAY MORNING I was surprised to see Ben roll up in front of the apartment. He didn't come up to the door, just honked his horn. I went down and got in.

"Hi," I said.

He didn't say anything. There was something frigid about the atmosphere in the car. We drove downtown, and he stopped about a block from the sheriff's department.

"What's going on?" I said.

He didn't speak, just pointed.

Two cruisers were pulling up in front of the sheriff's department. Walking down the path from the front door of the office was Ben's dad. His hands were cuffed to a wide leather belt around his waist, and his feet were shackled so that he had to shuffle as he walked. Two big deputies flanked him, holding his arms.

"Okay, you've seen it, Chass," Ben whispered. "Now get out of my car."

"But . . ."

"*You* did this," he said. "*You* did this to my dad. Get out, please."

I didn't move.

"Get. Out." His jaw was clenched and his mouth was a hard line. But there were tears running down his face in two wet streams. He reached across me and yanked open the door. Then he pushed me.

I didn't feel anything when he touched me. No *ksssshshhh*, no nothing. I just felt empty as I got out of the car.

Ben slammed the door.

"Don't come to my house," he said. "I don't care where you go, where you sleep, what you do anymore. Just don't do it anywhere near me."

"I'm sorry, Ben," I said. I could feel tears welling up in my eyes. "I didn't mean it to happen like this."

"You and your precious mom," he said. "You don't care about anything else except your little world."

Then he hung a U-turn and drove swiftly back down the road toward school.

TWENTY-THREE

AFTER BEN DROVE off, the sheriff saw me. He walked down to where I was standing and said, "So. You happy now?"

"What?" I said.

He was wearing his usual power suit, but his tie was pulled down a little and his blond hair wasn't quite as perfect as it usually was. "Addison Purvis came down and confessed to killing Nancy Rydel."

"Did he mention how she ended up in that basement? How some friends of his had helped him?"

The sheriff looked off toward the end of the street, shook his head finally. "Nah." He laughed without any sort of smile showing up on his face. "Addison's not that kind of guy. Don't know if I'd have been so generous if I'd been in his shoes. Probably would have sold out everybody I knew to save getting myself put in jail."

I studied his face and wondered if it was true. He had an expression on his face like he didn't like himself much.

"Anyway," he said, "you're off the hook. He made me agree not to charge you with anything."

"If you see him, thank him for me," I said.

"I'm still handing you over to DHR tomorrow morning at nine o'clock sharp," he said. "The paperwork's already gone through."

"Maybe my mother will be back by then," I said.

He seemed to be looking right through me. "Just try not to ruin anybody else's life between now and then," he said finally. Then he turned and walked away.

TWENTY-FOUR

I WENT BACK to my house to catch the school bus. As I was heading down the path outside our apartment, I noticed our mailbox was full. I hadn't checked it for a week. I opened the box, and there was so much stuff jammed in there—mostly bills and junk mail—that it was practically spilling out onto the ground. So much stuff, in fact, that I almost missed it.

There, all the way in the back of the mailbox, was a small key.

I pulled it out, stared at it. It was an odd-looking key, flat, longer than a normal door key, with lots of complicated ridges cut in it. I'd seen one before. It was a safe-deposit box key. A couple of times when we'd move to a new town, Mom would get a safe-deposit box at a bank. Not always, but sometimes.

A bank. The address on the advertisement was for the Planters and Southern Bank. So maybe Mom hadn't meant to meet me there at all. Maybe she just meant to point out to me which bank this key was for.

I held the key in my hand and stood there on the side of the road, staring. It felt hot in my hand for some reason.

The school bus pulled up. One of the kids stuck her head out and said, "Chass! What time's your show, huh?"

I kept staring at the key.

"You getting on or not?" the bus driver said.

After a minute I said, "Not."

Then I turned and started walking down the street toward the center of town.

"Chass! Dude! What time's your show?"

The manager of the bank was an old guy with gray hair and a green polyester suit.

I showed him the key and said, "I don't know if you know who I am, but my mom has disappeared, and she left me this key. I think it's to a safe-deposit box."

The manager said, "How about you come back in my office, hon."

We went back and sat down. He clicked some keys on his computer and said, "Allison Pureheart? She's your mama, right?"

I nodded.

He made a clicking sound with his lips. "See, thing is, she's the only authorized signatory to the box."

"What's that mean?"

"It means I can't let you in without court authorization."

"How would that work?"

"Well. I'd have to have an order from a probate judge."

"How do you get that?"

"Well, probate is what happens to the estate of a person after they, ah . . ." He cleared his throat.

"Die?"

He avoided my eye. "After they, yeah, after they pass away."

"Mom is missing. So far as I know, she's not dead. But what happens if nobody ever finds her? Whatever's in that box—are you telling me it's going to sit there forever?"

"Well . . ."

"Surely in a situation like this there's some kind of procedure. I mean, she left me a note telling me to open the box and everything."

The bank manager rubbed his palms up and down his thighs a couple of times. He sighed loudly. "Can you show me the note?"

"It's at home."

He eyed me for a minute.

"This is a small town," I said. "I mean, you know who I am, right? Everybody knows my mom is missing. Everybody knows I'm all by myself and I . . ." I hesitated. He had the look of the sort of guy who would have a hard time saying no to a crying girl. I thought about faking it. And then suddenly it hit me. This wasn't a fake situation. It wasn't like I was trying to put something over on him. I really *was* a sixteen-year-old girl, alone in the world, who needed to get into that safe-deposit box.

I started bawling.

"Now look, honey . . . " he said. "Sweetheart, I know you're upset, but . . ."

I put my head in my hands and just sat there crying. After a minute he stood up. Attached to his belt was a jingling ring of keys. They looked more like something a janitor would wear than a bank manager.

"I know I shouldn't," he said. He pulled one of the keys off and held it up in front of me.

An hour later I was sitting at the kitchen table of our apartment, staring at a shoe box wrapped with gobs of knotted string. The shoe box had been the only thing inside of the safe-deposit box at the bank. I cut it open with a kitchen knife and took off the lid.

Inside were a couple of old, yellowed newspaper articles and a smaller, square box that said MEMOREX on the top. I recognized the articles. They were the same ones I'd seen before about the boating accident in which Jimmy Laws had died.

I opened the flat cardboard box. Inside was a big reel of recording tape. I recognized it as the sort of tape that used to be used to record music in professional recording studios in the old days back before computers.

Attached to the tape reel was a note. It read:

> *To whom it may concern. This tape constitutes evidence of a murder. The relevant portions of the recording can be found starting fourteen minutes and thirty seconds into the tape.*

The note was signed *Jenna Farmer*.

Jenna Farmer. I thought I recognized the name, but still I had to check. I pulled out the sheaf of fake ID cards with Mom's pictures on them. The name on the backstage pass to Madison Square Garden—it was Jenna Farmer.

Oh my God, I thought. *That's it. That's Mom's real name.*

I picked up the box, walked out the door, started heading toward the library.

Ten minutes later I was talking to Mr. Percival, the reference librarian. "I know I keep bugging you, but can I see that album of information about Jimmy Laws?"

Mr. Percival smiled at me. "No trouble, Chass," he said. He went around the desk, pulled out the heavy album, and handed it to me.

I flipped to a page near the end, looked at it more carefully. "Didn't I see that you had a program from his last concert? Or something like that?"

"Not a program," he said. "It was just a concert announcement from the *New York Times*." He stood beside me, turned several pages. "Oh. Here."

The announcement was very small—just a couple of lines.

SAT. POP ROCKER JIMMY LAWS. 8:30. MADISON SQ. GDN. OPENING ACT— SINGER/SONGWRITER JENNA FARMER.

There was a picture of Jimmy on the facing page, a picture that had obviously been taken at the concert. He had his arm around a laughing young woman whose face was obscured by her hair. My heart was suddenly racing. I had looked at the picture before, but I hadn't looked at it carefully. The young woman Jimmy was holding onto—I couldn't see her face. But there was something about her body, her hands, her neck. Suddenly I realized: *It was Mom.*

"Are you all right?" Mr. Percival said.

"What?"

"Are you all right? Your face just turned white."

I touched the picture with my fingertips.

"What do you know about her, Mr. Percival?"

He shrugged. "He was always popular with the girls," Mr. Percival said wistfully.

I had been thinking about it for a while, but suddenly I asked myself the question square on. Had Mom been Jimmy Laws's girlfriend? Or, to put it more bluntly: Was Jimmy Laws my father?

"Do you think I look like Jimmy?" I said.

Mr. Percival frowned. "What kind of question is that?"

"Just answer me," I said. "Please."

He squinted, stared at my face. "Y'all both have blond hair, snub noses . . ."

My cell phone rang.

"Hello?"

"Chass!" An enthusiastic male voice. "It's Justin Taylor at Iambic Records. I'm over in Atlanta, just checking to see if your gig is still on for tonight."

"Uh, yeah, absolutely," I said.

"You said it's an early show, right? Eight-thirty?"

"Uh-huh."

"Listened to your demo on the way out," he said. "I'm totally digging it. I got some ideas I want to bounce off you, a couple things that might tighten it up lyrically. Are you cool with that?"

"Uh. Sure."

"Right on. See ya tonight."

I hung up, looked at my watch. Ten-fifteen. I was supposed to be in American history. Not that I had any way to get out to the school now. According to Mrs. Oglesby, the woman from the state DHR, I was going to be picked up tomorrow at nine. That gave me less than twenty-four hours to find Mom.

School was going to have to wait.

"Thanks, Mr. Percival," I said. And I ran out of the library, clutching my precious shoe box.

TWENTY-FIVE

A FEW MINUTES later I was on the front porch of a grubby little white frame house over near the old cotton mill. It was owned by Doug Slayton, Ben's friend who had helped me record the demo that had ended up at Iambic Records. I banged loudly on the front door.

Nobody answered.

I banged some more.

Finally the door opened, and a sleepy-looking guy with long stringy hair looked out at me. "Dude," he said. "What time is it?"

"Late enough, Doug," I said. I pushed past him into his disaster area of a living room.

"Dude, I was sleeping. I was up till like four in the morning working on some mix tapes."

I plunked the shoe box on the table, opened it, pulled out the box that said MEMOREX on the side, and handed it to him.

"I need to listen to this," I said. "Can you help me?"

He held up his hands helplessly. "Look, Chass, okay, it's like early? And I need some sustenance. Okay? Before I use my brain and everything?"

"Fine."

He went into his kitchen and poured a bowl of Count Chocula, came back, swept a bunch of magazines and science fiction novels off the table and onto the floor, then sat down and ate the cereal in silence.

When he was done, he clapped his hands. "All better. Lemme check out that tape."

He opened the flat box, pulled out the reel-to-reel tape.

"Dog!" he said. "Two-inch tape. You don't see much of this anymore."

"How can I listen to it?"

"Well, see, you'd have to have a two-inch tape recorder. Buy one new, you're talking fifty thousand bucks. Very rare items. Nowadays you'd probably have to go to Atlanta or Nashville to find one of these."

I felt deflated. "Oh, man," I said. "I'm screwed."

Doug looked at me for a minute then grinned. "Unless, of course, you have a friend who has a studio in his house and collects fine vintage recording equipment."

I gave him a hug. "Doug! You are the greatest!"

"I know, I know," he said. "It's true."

He led me back through the wreckage of his house into the room he used as a studio. As we walked through the studio door, it was as though we had entered an entirely different building, inhabited by an entirely different person. The room was full of gleaming equipment, everything neat and spotless and filed away.

He walked to the corner of the room, pulled a plastic dustcover off an electronic device.

"*Voilà!*" he said. "Behold, the Ampex MM-1200. In its day, the finest twenty-four-track recorder in the world. This very recorder was used to record 'In Memory of Elizabeth Reed' by the Allman Brothers, 'Sweet Home Alabama' by Lynyrd Skynyrd, and 'Mindbender' by Grinderswitch."

"Grinderswitch?" I said. "Who's Grinderswitch?"

He sighed loudly. "What's the world coming to? Your generation is so pathetically ignorant. I bet you think Britney Spears is Old School."

"*My* generation? I'm like four years younger than you."

"My point exactly." Doug grinned smugly. "Give me that tape."

He threaded it expertly into the machine, connected some wires in the back, and then hit the PLAY button.

A male voice came out of the speakers on the wall. "This is Airways Studio tape number three-forty-one, recording May fourteenth. The artist is Jenna Farmer and the song is 'If You Really Knew Me.'"

A song began playing. It was a woman singing. The song was sad, about a girl misunderstood by her boyfriend.

Doug fiddled around with the sliders on his huge mixing board, and the voice came farther out of the mix.

"Jenna Farmer," he said. "Who's Jenna Farmer?"

"It's my mother," I said.

His eyes widened. "This is your *mom*? Whoa! Man, she's pretty good." He hit the STOP button, rewound it, fiddled around with all his equipment, and then started the tape again.

I closed my eyes and let the song wash over me. Pretty soon I had tears running down my face. I couldn't tell if it was because the song was such a tearjerker or because it was so sad that Mom had given all of this up. I couldn't make sense of it. Why would a person give up on a talent like that?

After the song was over, Doug flipped the machine off.

"No, wait," I said. "The thing I wanted to listen to— it's about fourteen minutes in."

Doug frowned then hit the PLAY button. There was a moment or two of silence, and then suddenly a man began talking. He had a strong southern accent, and he sounded tired. He was complaining about something to do with his tour bus being broken down.

Then a woman's voice interrupted him. The woman said, "Is that why you came here, Jimmy? To whine about your tour bus?" Her voice sounded younger than the one I was used to—but was obviously Mom.

The man—it must have been Jimmy Laws—said, "Yeah, well, you know . . ."

"No, I don't know, Jimmy." Mom sounded irritated at Jimmy, like maybe they had been fighting or something.

Jimmy rambled on some more, telling a couple of stories about people who were obviously familiar to both of them but who meant nothing to me. The whole time he was talking, I kept hearing ice clinking in a glass.

"Jimmy," Mom said, "if you keep drinking like that, you're going to pass out and Nick or I will have to drive you home again."

"I'm fine," Jimmy said.

There was a long silence. Finally Jimmy Laws said, "I don't know what to do."

"About . . ."

Another long pause. A clinking of ice, then a loud sigh. "I was raised okay," Jimmy said. "I mean my old man was a little stricter than necessary, but I went to church every Sunday, every Wednesday night. But there's something wrong with me."

"Jimmy, it's getting late. Spit it out. I've been singing all day, I'm tired, I need to get home and sleep."

Again, a long pause. Finally Jimmy said, "You remember that girl Angelica?"

"Angelica?"

"Angelica Robinson. She was hanging around a lot when I was cutting the record back in January."

Mom's tone was flat, dry. "The really dumb, really eager one with the big chest and the—"

"Yeah, yeah, yeah, you don't have to rub it in. Anyway, one day when we were taking a break from the record, Kyle said why don't we go to his house in the Hamptons."

"Kyle Van Epps."

"Sure. Anyway, we go out to his place, and this girl, Angelica, she tags along."

"You, Kyle, and Angelica. That must have been fun."

"And, of course, Kyle brings out some party favors. We sit out on the deck behind his house looking at the water. I get a little overexcited on the party favors, and one thing leads to another." More clinking of ice. "Only Angelica, suddenly she's acting like little Miss Innocent. Like she didn't know what we were out there for. Well,

Kyle, he gets pissed when she says she's not interested, and he pushes her down on the deck and says, 'Jimmy, why don't you give her some instruction.' I'm like, 'Instruction in what?' He goes, 'Oh, come on, you know what I mean.'"

"And then?"

"I didn't do anything. So Kyle goes, 'All right, then I'll do it.' And he just slaps her, whap, right upside the head."

The tape was silent for a long time.

Finally Mom said, "And then?"

"She spit right in my face. I go, 'What's that for?' She goes, 'That's for letting him do it.' I just kind of looked at her. I must have grinned or laughed or something, because she smacked me in the face, just like he'd done to her. And I just got mad, and I hit her. I hit her about five times, bam bam bam bam bam. And she starts wailing, and then I just kept hitting her till she shut up."

"Jimmy! My God!"

"I know, I know."

"What did you do then?"

"I got a little spooked, so I propped her up in a chair, felt for her pulse. She was still alive. I said to Kyle, 'Man, we gotta call an ambulance.' After a couple seconds Kyle goes back inside the house. I figure he's calling nine-one-

one, but instead he comes out with the keys to his boat. Then he's like, 'Let's go.' And I'm like, 'Where?' He says, 'Out.' So he picks her up, and we go down, get on his boat, and off we go into Long Island Sound. After a while Angelica comes around. She's beat up pretty bad, but you can see she's gonna be okay. She asks where we're going. But Kyle just ignores her.

"Anyway, we get out into the sound a ways, where we're not close to anybody, and Kyle goes, 'Hey, Jimmy, hand me that thing over there.' It was one of those things they have on boats. Like a spike? With a hook on the end?"

"A marlinespike." It was Mom's voice, quiet.

"Yeah. A marlinespike. So I hand it to him. And Angelica's just looking at it, then looking at Kyle. And she goes, 'What are you doing?' And Kyle doesn't say anything. He just takes that marlinespike like a baseball bat, and it's like, *ka-pow*, right in her head."

"I'm not sure I want to hear the rest of this, Jimmy."

"I'm like, 'Kyle, what are you doing?' And he hits her a couple more times. Then he goes, 'Man, you just about killed her. You have any interest in going to jail for the next five, six years?' I'm like, 'No.' And he's like, 'Well, there you are then. Because that's how long you'd be there if she went to the cops.'"

There was some stirring around.

"I don't remember the rest too good. I was drinking a lot that night. But Kyle—you know how he is. Always real businesslike, no matter what. He rubs his hands together and says, 'Okay, now we make her go away.' And we, uh, we tied her up and rigged some weights to her and some chain and stuff, and Kyle drove the boat out about five miles into the ocean, and we just pushed her overboard. Boom. No more Angelica."

The tape was silent again.

"What's wrong with me?" Jimmy said. "Why does this stuff keep happening?"

"What do you mean? Something like this has happened before?"

Another pause. "I, uh . . . Well . . ."

"Oh, God, no, Jimmy . . ."

"Back in high school. Me and some buddies, we were over at this friend of mine's house. Same kind of deal. Girl's at the house. Seems like she's the type that's ready, willing, and able. Only when you . . . when the crunch comes, so to speak, she's not interested. She gets weird, she gets pissy."

"Jimmy . . ."

"I killed her, man. I just got mad and I beat the crap out of her. And then I let this buddy of mine think he'd done it. He'd fallen asleep, and I just rubbed some blood on his knuckles. His name was Addison. Anyway when Addison woke up, he's got blood all over his hands, and the girl's lying there . . . I let him think he'd had too much to drink and blacked out. Like he'd done it himself."

"What happened to him?"

"Nothing. We buried the girl. The three of us. This buddy of mine, Addison, his old man was a big cheese in town. And the other friend, his dad was the sheriff. Addison's daddy and the sheriff, they made sure nothing happened to Addison."

There was a long, long, long silence. Finally my mother said, "Jimmy, you do what you want. I'm not telling you what to do. But I don't want to see your face again. Not ever."

"I'm gonna come clean."

"I don't care, I—"

"I'm gonna go to that cop. There was a cop, the one that handled Angelica's disappearance. He was suspicious. But he didn't have anything on us. Angelica hadn't told anybody she was coming with us. It was a last-minute thing. There was no body. But I'm gonna go to the cops."

"I'm just going to give you one piece of advice."

"Yeah?"

"Don't tell Kyle about this. If he killed that girl, he'd kill you too."

"Why would I tell Kyle?"

There was a long silence, and then the tape ran out, the end of the tape spinning and flipping as the reel continued to spin.

"Okay," Doug said, turning off the reel-to-reel recorder, "I'm awake now."

TWENTY-SIX

I TOOK THE tape from Doug and started walking back downtown. I knew I had to bring it straight to Sheriff Arnett. I was feeling so crappy about being responsible for Ben's dad getting put in jail, that I wanted to make things right as quickly as I could.

I tried Ben's cell, but of course he was in trig, so he didn't answer.

I decided to send him an e-mail, just in case he managed to log on during study hall. I logged on from my cell, found a bunch of messages in my box. There was

one message from Mr. Winbush (It has come to my attention that you are absent. An attempt has been made without success to contact your parents. If you fail to bring a
signed excuse from your parent or guardian, you will be
marked UNEXCUSED. As per state regulations, more than
five unexcused absences in one calendar year . . . blah
blah blah). I also had a couple of messages from kids asking if I could sneak them into the show that night. But
the last message almost made my heart stop.

It said:

Bugaboo,
Sorry about disappearing on you. I'll never do
it again. Meet me after your show at that bar
tonight at midnight and I'll explain everything.
I have a lot of things to tell you. Bring the tape
(you know which one I mean). I'll be meeting
someone tonight who will help us. This will all
be over soon, I promise. I love you.
Mom
P.S. Don't tell ANYONE that you heard from me
or that you have the tape!

I stared at the screen of my cell phone. Could it be
some kind of ruse? I didn't think so. Who else would
know that Mom called me Bugaboo?

I felt like laughing and crying all at once. I stopped in the middle of the road and whooped. Some old dude in a pickup truck was driving by. He looked out the window at me like I was crazy.

I waved both my arms at him. He frowned and slowed his truck down.

"You all right, girl?" he said.

"Never been better in my life."

"You look a little funny is all."

Just ten minutes ago, I didn't think twice about cutting school. But now that Mom was going to be coming back, all of a sudden it was like my perspective shifted and I was normal again. I had this huge sense of like *Oh crap, I should be at school!*

My intention had been to take the tape straight to Sheriff Arnett. But Mom's message made it clear I shouldn't do that.

So I said to the old guy in the truck: "I kind of missed the bus, and my mom's out of town. I don't suppose you could take me out to the high school."

"Sure, darlin'," he said.

When I got to school, kids kept coming up to me in the hall and flashing fake ID cards and grinning at me. I grinned right back. I don't think I'd grinned so hard in all my life.

At lunchtime I saw Brittany and Ben sitting together. They were at the table where all the cheerleaders and jocks sat. I had never sat at that table in my life—and I'm sure Ben hadn't either. It made me feel all weird seeing him there. Ben was talking, and his eyes were looking at the floor. Brittany was listening, and her eyes were on Ben's face. I'm sure he was probably talking about what had happened to his dad that morning. She reached out and put her hand on his. I felt—I don't know if *jealous* is the right word—but I felt mad, seeing her touch him like that.

Mom's message had said not to tell anybody about the tape—but I figured I owed it to him to tell him that I had proof his dad didn't kill Nancy Rydel.

I pulled a chair over from the next table and sat down.

"There's something I have to tell you, Ben," I said.

He looked at me for a second then picked up his tray, stood up, and walked away.

Brittany looked at me for a minute then said, "Aren't you at the wrong table?"

"I guess I must be."

I got up and went over to where Ben had sat, off in the corner at a table by himself. When I sat down, he got up and went back over to the table with all the popular people.

"Ben!" I yelled. "Please!"

Everybody was staring at us. Ben didn't even look at me. It was so humiliating.

I put my head down and finished my meal by myself. I kept taking out my cell phone and looking at the message from Mom, mulling it over.

Why would she want to meet me at Ronnie's? It seemed odd. If I'd gotten the message a week ago, I wouldn't have believed it. Meeting me at a bar? Where they play music? Not in a million years. But that was before I found out that my music-hating mother had once been a professional musician. She'd probably snuck into bars when she was sixteen too.

Well, whatever was going to happen—it was going to go down at Ronnie's that night. If the message was real, this whole nightmare would be over around midnight.

TWENTY-SEVEN

AFTER I GOT home from school, I walked over to Doug Slayton's house to ask if I could borrow a PA system and a microphone for the show that night. He didn't answer the door. I got a little bit of a panicky feeling. We had agreed that morning that he was going to loan it to me, and that he would be there in the afternoon to show me how it worked. If I didn't have a PA, I was going to be screwed.

His car was still there, though, so I figured maybe he

was in his soundproofed studio and just couldn't hear me. The door wasn't locked, so I just walked in.

"Doug? Hey, Doug?"

No answer. The living room seemed even more trashed than it had been that morning. The place was such a wreck that it took me a second to figure it out: The coffee table was broken, and a chair had been turned over. This wasn't just messy housekeeping. Suddenly I was feeling very scared.

I went over to the door of Doug's studio and pushed it open.

What I saw made me sick. Doug's beautiful studio, with its thousands and thousands of dollars' worth of equipment, had been totally destroyed. There were amps turned over, knobs torn off, black electronics boxes lying on the floor with their covers smashed, a computer with a hammer handle sticking out of the broken monitor screen.

And Doug himself lay on the floor. His hands were behind his back, cuffed to the old iron radiator, and a bunch of duct tape was wrapped around his head, covering his mouth. He was still moving, at least. He turned and looked at me with this scared expression on his face.

I ran over and peeled the duct tape off his mouth. He had a bruise over one eye, and his lip was cut and swollen.

"What happened?" I said.

"What did you get me into, dude?" he said. "Look at it! They smashed it all!"

"Who did?"

"Two guys. Big bodybuilder-looking assholes. They had guns."

"Was one of them Asian?"

He frowned. "Asian? Nah, dude, they were just regular old white guys."

"What did they want?"

"They wanted the tape. I tried to pretend I didn't know what they were talking about but . . ." He looked at the floor. "They kinda busted me up and I got scared. I thought . . . I thought they were gonna . . ."

"I know, I know, it's okay."

"There's some bolt cutters in the garage. Can you get me outta here?"

I went out to the garage, got the bolt cutters, came back, and cut the chain attaching the cuffs together. He shook his arms then stood up unsteadily.

"I made a CD of the tape," he said. "But they got it."

"Don't worry about it," I said.

He looked at me for a long moment, like he was trying to tell me something, or trying to decide something. Then he said, "What did you do with the tape?"

"It's cool," I said. "It's right here in my backpack."

A funny look came across his face, like maybe he was a little disappointed.

"What?" I said.

Then I saw that he was looking over my shoulder at something behind me.

I turned, and there were three men standing in the middle of the living room—two big ones and one older guy in a fancy-looking suit. The older guy had a goatee and a shaved head, like he was trying to look younger and hipper than he really was.

"I'm impressed," the man said. He had a rich, smoky voice, like a radio announcer. "You've done marvelously for a sixteen-year-old girl. But it's time to give me the tape."

"Who are you?" I said.

"My name is Kyle Van Epps," he said. Then he reached under his jacket and pulled out a pistol, pointed it at my head.

"My name is Chastity," I said.

"No, actually your name is Darcy Farmer. Now give me the tape."

Darcy Farmer. I stared at Kyle Van Epps for a long time. Darcy Farmer? That didn't seem like my name at all. All kinds of stuff was swirling around in my head.

Including the unfairness of finding out my real name from the very person who'd robbed it from me in the first place. It just didn't sink in.

"Let's go, sweetie. The tape." He snapped his fingers at me like I was a waitress who'd forgotten his coffee. Mom used to talk about guys doing that, snapping their fingers at her, how it bugged her worse than anything in the world.

You don't really plan things in a situation like this. You just *do* stuff. If I'd had any sense, I guess I would have just given him the tape.

But I didn't. Instead, I stepped into the living room and swung the bolt cutters. They were three feet long, with huge steel jaws and long steel handles. They probably weighed like ten pounds.

The bolt cutters smashed into Kyle Van Epps's hand, and the gun went flying up in the air.

"That bitch broke my hand!" Kyle Van Epps howled. "Get in there and kill her."

The two big guys behind him pulled out their pistols and hurled themselves at me.

But before they could reach me, I stepped back into the studio, slammed the door, and locked it.

If it had been any kind of normal door, those two huge guys would have smashed it right off the hinges. But it wasn't. Because it was a studio door, designed to be soundproof, it was extra heavy wood, reinforced around the edges so the sound wouldn't leak in while Doug was recording. There was a very, very muffled boom as one of them banged into the door, but that was all.

I pulled out my cell phone, called 911, handed the phone to Doug, and said, "Talk to them. Just do me a favor and don't mention I'm here."

Doug had an intercom with a small TV screen in it next to the door. That way he could see who was outside and talk to them when he was recording. I flipped it on. On the screen I could see one of the big guys smashing repeatedly into the door.

I punched the TALK button on the small white box next to the door and said, "Hey, Mr. Van Epps. I just called the cops. I don't know how it is out in L.A. Maybe the cops can get stuck in traffic, take all night to get to you. But here it takes about a minute to get from the sheriff's office to anyplace in town. If I were you, I'd hit the road."

There was a pause, then Kyle Van Epps stepped toward the intercom box on the other side of the wall, stuck his face right up to the camera, and smiled this big mean smile. "Don't get to feeling comfortable, sweet thing. One way or another, that tape is mine."

Then he motioned to the other two men to follow him, and they disappeared out the front door.

Doug handed me my cell. "Sheriff's on the way," he said.

"Good."

He looked away from me. "I'm sorry, Chass. They had guns. They said they'd kill me. I told them that you were coming, and they said to just wait and they'd hide in the other room, and I was supposed to ask you about the tape and—"

"Doug," I interrupted. "Forget it. Anybody would have done the same thing."

He sighed. "*You* wouldn't have, Chass."

We stood there awkwardly for a minute.

"So. Chass. You still need that PA system for tonight?"

I laughed. Something about it seemed hilarious, talking about PA systems when we'd both just about been killed only half a minute earlier. "If it's not too much trouble."

"Hey," Doug said, smiling wanly, "I owe you."

I gave him a hug. "You don't owe me anything."

I looked over at the intercom on the wall. A sheriff's deputy appeared, yelling something that we couldn't hear.

"I'm gone," I said. "When the sheriff asks, some crazy guys were just trying to steal your studio equipment. Don't mention the tape."

He frowned. "Okay. But how are you going to explain to them about your—"

"Me?" I said. "That's the thing, see, I was never even here."

I opened the back door to his studio. It led into his yard. I closed the door gently and ran across Doug's weedy backyard, heading for the fence.

TWENTY-EIGHT

OUT BY THE river on the south side of town there was an abandoned cotton mill where Ben and I used to go and mess around in the summer. I lugged my guitar down there and hid out, practicing nervously all afternoon. But I wasn't thinking much about the music. Instead I kept thinking about what Kyle Van Epps had said—that my real name was Darcy Farmer.

I didn't feel like a Darcy. I realized that I had been Chass Pureheart for three years now—longer than any other name I'd had. It felt more like *me* than my real name did.

Around six, I closed my guitar case. There was a loose brick in the back wall of the mill where Ben and I used to hide things. I pulled out the brick and hid the tape with Jimmy Laws's confession on it. Was my father a murderer? No wonder Mom had never told me anything about him.

All my life there had been all these mysteries. After a while you start to build up expectations about what's behind them, fantasies about what your real life was supposed to be like. And now that the veil was finally being torn off, I was starting to feel like I didn't really want to know after all. Maybe sometimes it was better not to know the truth about things. It all seemed so cheap and ugly.

And on top of it all, I was losing Ben.

I realized I'd been taking him for granted for a long time. Now that I was losing him, I wished that I could go back and change it, that I could have at least kissed him one time or made out with him in the Batmobile or something. I was feeling all mixed up.

After I'd hidden the tape, I picked up my guitar case and walked slowly through the town. Suppose Mom's e-mail was right? Suppose she had figured something out that was going to allow us to stop running? What then? Would we stay here?

It wasn't much of a town. There wasn't much of a reason for us to stay. And yet it felt more like home than anyplace I'd ever been. I had a sad, wistful feeling as I walked past the old houses that dated back to around the Civil War, the brick businesses that lined the main drag of town, the statue of the Confederate soldier with all the pigeons pooping on his hat.

The shadows were getting long as I walked into Norma's Café on the square. Across the street I saw a black SUV with heavily tinted windows. Wong. I still didn't know what he wanted, or whether I could trust him. Farther down was a yellow Hummer with two men in front and one in back. I had a hunch it was Kyle Van Epps. They were waiting. I figured I'd be okay as long as I stayed in a crowd.

I ordered a meal—fried chicken, corn bread, turnip greens, mac and cheese.

It was all coming down. Whatever my life was really about, it was all going to come clear tonight.

When I was done, I had a piece of rhubarb pie. I put the last money I had in the world down on the counter as I left. Seven dollars and thirty-one cents. Then I walked to the front door, took a deep breath, and walked out into the twilight.

TWENTY-NINE

MY FIRST GIG.

I'd always imagined a huge stage, screaming fans, lights, smoke, a backup band full of cute guys with cool tattoos—all that stuff. Instead I walked into Ronnie's, and the stage consisted of a six-inch-high piece of plywood perched on top of some paint cans. It smelled like beer and cigarettes, and the only members of the audience were a couple of old rednecks hunched over at the bar. Otherwise the place was empty.

The owner, Lon What's-his-name, was sitting behind

the bar watching this stupid reality TV show where all these bitchy but ridiculously beautiful women try to get this fat dumb guy to marry them so they can win a bunch of money.

"Um," I said, "I'm here to play tonight?"

Lon What's-his-name looked at me and said, "Huh?"

"Remember? Chass Pureheart? You said I could play here tonight?"

He squinted at me, his mouth slightly open. "Play *what*?"

"Music." I held up my guitar case.

"We don't have no live music here," he said.

I felt my face flush. "I gave you twenty-five bucks! You said I could play!"

"I don't remember nothing about that." He shrugged, turned back to the TV.

"But—" I felt sick. What if everybody showed up—including the guy from Iambic Records—and I wasn't even there to play! Suddenly I wanted to crawl in a hole and die.

After a minute Lon What's-his-name turned back around and winked at me. "I'm just fooling with you, hon," he said. He pointed lackadaisically toward the far corner of the bar. "Your buddy came over a while back, dropped off the PA system. You can set up over there."

Relief flooded through me. "God, you about gave me a heart attack!"

He smiled, showing off a bunch of holes where teeth were supposed to be. "Since you gave me twenty-five bucks," he said, "your drinks are on me." Then he poured a beer, pushed the foam off the top with a greasy steak knife, and slid it across the bar. I stared at it for a minute, waiting for him to ask me for an ID. But all he did was turn back to the TV and start watching all the bitchy women in their low-cut ballroom dresses.

I couldn't believe it. After I'd been nearly killed getting that fake ID up in Birmingham, the guy didn't even bother to check it. I didn't want to look like some dumb kid who'd never been in a bar, so I picked up the beer and walked across the room. Out of curiosity I took a sip. It tasted like crap. How could people drink that stuff?

It took me about fifteen minutes to set up the PA system. I had no idea how it worked or what plugged into what. There were speakers and an amplifier and lots and lots wires and all kinds of different plugs with different holes.

But finally I got it working. My guitar was plugged in, my mic was on—everything was ready. I looked at my watch. Eight-thirty, showtime.

Then I looked around the room. It was me, the two

burnt-out old rednecks, and Lon the bartender. Where was the crowd? Where were all the people who'd said they were coming? Where were all the kids who said they'd been getting fake IDs off the Web? Had it all been a big joke at my expense?

"Hi, everybody," I said. The two rednecks at the bar kept talking, their backs to me. Lon kept watching the TV. "This is a song by Dashboard Confessional. It's called 'The Sharp Hint of New Tears.'"

I started to play. No one even glanced at me. I pretty much wanted to shoot myself.

THIRTY

I **PLAYED FOR** about forty-five minutes. A couple of beefy women who looked like they might be truck drivers came in and played pool. When I finished one song, one of them looked up and yelled, "Hey, doll, you know anything by Reba McEntire?"

"Gosh, you know, I sure don't," I said.

"Well, the hell with you," she said. Then she turned around and sank the eight ball.

I kept singing, but all I could think was *So this is*

what I wanted to do with my life. No wonder Mom tried to keep me away from it.

After a while I stopped even looking out at the room. I just stared at the floor and sang, trying to ignore everything. The whole time I had this terrible sinking feeling. What would that guy from Iambic Records think when he showed up and there was nobody here? He'd think I was the world's biggest loser.

Eventually I played this new song I'd written called "You Tear Everything Down."

When I was done, I heard someone applauding, one lonely pair of hands echoing through the room. I looked back into the dim bar, and for a minute I couldn't make out who it was.

Then I saw. It was that kid Jay-Jay Brice, the one who got caught selling fake IDs to everybody.

He just kept clapping and clapping and clapping. After a minute I started laughing. I put my mouth up to the microphone and said, "Okay, guys, I'm taking a five-minute break. I'll be back at nine-thirty."

I put down my guitar, walked over and said, "So you're my entire fan club, huh?"

"Hey, just chillin'," he said. Jay-Jay was leaning on the bar, trying to look all mature and everything. It was pretty funny. He looked around the room. "This kinda sucks, huh, dude?"

I laughed. "Yeah. But thanks for coming."

He shrugged. "Hey, you kicked ass at the talent show back in the fall. Had to come check it out. That last song rocked."

"Thanks," I said. I hesitated. "You haven't seen Ben anywhere, have you?"

"Ben?"

"You know. Ben."

"Oh. Yeah. *That* Ben."

"Is there another one?"

"Yeah. Ben. Yeah. No." For a moment he looked vaguely uncomfortable. "I heard he was going out with Brittany Arnett tonight. They went to one of them make-out movies, you know what I'm saying. I hate those kinda movies. Everybody kissing and licking on each other?" He did something vulgar with his tongue. "Dude, if it don't got explosions or naked chicks, I can't be wasting my time."

I didn't say anything.

"So, you and Ben," he said. "You and him weren't . . . like . . ."

"Nah," I said. "Nah." But I was feeling half-sick all of a sudden.

"Cool." He sighed loudly. " 'Cause I got to tell you, once a dude dates a cheerleader, he never goes back to normal girls." He turned to Lon, the bartender. "Hey, bro, could I get a drink down here?"

After a minute, Lon turned away from the TV. "What you want?"

"Uh . . ." Jay-Jay had a comically guilty look on his face. "How about a rum and Coke?"

Lon look at him with a flat, humorless gaze. "How about *not*, son?"

"What?" Jay-Jay said.

"That was the most bogus-looking ID I ever seen in my life, boy. I don't mind letting you watch your friend here, but I ain't dumb enough to be serving you no alcohol."

"Okay. Gimme a Mr. Pibb." Jay-Jay turned back to me. "Man! What's *up* with that dude?"

"Well, you got to admit," I said, "you're only a sophomore in high school."

Jay-Jay looked around the room. "Dude, this really sucks. This *really* sucks."

"Don't leave," I said. "Please."

He looked at me quizzically. "*Leaving*? Who said anything about leaving?"

I looked over Jay-Jay's shoulder. It was already nine-thirty. Justin Taylor, the guy from Iambic records, still wasn't here. I wasn't sure whether I was more sorry or relieved. If the guy showed up and found me playing in this empty dump, he probably wouldn't know whether to laugh or get angry at me for wasting his time.

I went to the bathroom. When I came out, I found

that several more kids from school had arrived, some of Jay-Jay's doper buddies.

I got up on the rickety plywood stage again and sang for a while. Kids kept drifting in, showing their fake driver's licenses to the bartender, who was starting to look a little surprised by all the traffic. At first most of the kids were talking and playing pool and shoving each other and the usual stuff kids do. But by about the fifth song suddenly something happened that I couldn't explain. One minute nobody was paying much attention to me—and the next minute, they were. Just like that.

I played a song I'd written—the one that was on the demo I'd recorded at Doug Slayton's, the same one that Justin, the A&R guy from Iambic Records had heard—and when I was done suddenly everybody was clapping and whistling.

"I wrote that one," I said.

Jay-Jay was standing on a bar stool, yelling and clapping his hands over his head. Brandi Chun and a bunch of cheerleaders were there too. I still didn't see Ben. Or Brittany either for that matter.

But even so, I felt this sudden surge of warmth. It was like nothing I'd ever felt before. *Yes!* I thought. *This is it! This is what I wanted.*

I started singing this song I'd written a while back when I was in love with the quarterback of the football team, a senior named Warren Barry. Warren was standing in the back next to Brandi Chun and the cheerleader crowd. Funny thing—when I looked at him he just seemed so . . . ordinary. Suddenly, I could see Warren twenty years from now, selling real estate at his dad's real estate office, wearing the same polyester Sans-a-belt pants that his dad wore, and couldn't imagine how I was ever interested in somebody as boring as that.

No, right then there was only one person I wanted to sing that song to, and it was Ben. And now he was out on a date with Little Miss Perfect Bitch. What the hell had I been thinking all this time? It was totally obvious that he was interested in me, that he had been for a long time. And I had done nothing about it. What was I—crazy?

And now I'd blown it.

After I was done singing the song, the whole audience was quiet for a minute. They were just staring at me, like they couldn't believe some kid they knew could actually write a song that didn't totally suck.

Then they were all cheering and yelling and stomping, and then Jay-Jay started going *Chass Chass Chass Chass Chass!* and all the other kids started going *Chass Chass Chass*. Even Brandi Chun and Warren Barry and all their jerky popular friends joined in. It was just too weird. Three years I'm the world's biggest loser and then suddenly—*this*.

I played a couple more songs and took a break. As I was taking off my guitar, a stocky guy in a black T-shirt and jeans, his hair all gelled up in little dyed-blond points, walked up and stuck out his hand.

"Justin Taylor," he said. "From Iambic Records."

"Justin! Hi!" He gave me a big hug, like I was some old friend of his. He smelled like patchouli. "I was expecting somebody in a suit or something," I said when he finally let go of me.

He laughed like I was the funniest person in the world. "Dude, you are *killin'*. I'm serious. I can't believe the following you've got here. Look at these kids! You must have, what, almost a hundred people in here?" He waved his hands around the room. Kids were still coming in the front door. It seemed like half the school was there.

I shrugged, trying to act like it was no big deal, like I was used to this.

"I didn't recognize some of the stuff you were playing. How many of those songs did you write?"

"About half of them, I guess."

Justin stepped back, looked at me for a minute with a frank, appraising gaze. Then he made a little circle in the air. "Turn around for me, huh?"

I turned around, gave him a little flirty look over my shoulder, like I was some big model or something. It was the kind of thing I never do. But I was so pumped up from all the applause and everything that I just felt like I was on a roll. The record executive looked me up and down. I could tell he liked what he saw. The guy was like thirty—way too old to be checking out a high school girl. Tell you the truth, it made me feel a little uncomfortable.

He kept staring for a long time. Then suddenly he said, "Are you talking to any other labels?"

Talking to other labels. "You mean like to other record companies?"

"Yeah," he said impatiently. "Are you talking to any other record companies?"

"Not really, no."

"Good." He pointed his finger at me. "Do not move. Do not go anywhere. Okay? I got to make a phone call."

He whipped out a small, really expensive-looking cell phone and started talking excitedly to somebody. What was going on? It seemed like he was talking to somebody back in Los Angeles, like he really liked me and wanted to tell them about me.

Which was ridiculous, of course. That sort of thing doesn't happen in real life.

He was still talking on the phone when I started playing again. The kids didn't go quite as nuts as they had earlier, but still there was a lot of cheering and whistling. I noticed for the first half of the set that Justin Taylor was holding up his phone toward me, like he was letting somebody hear me. He would dial a number, talk, then hold up the phone for a while, then dial a new number and hold up the phone.

Meantime, I kept watching the door, hoping to see Ben's face.

After I finished my third set Jay-Jay came up to me and said, "So that dude back there? Is he from like some record company or something?"

"Yeah," I said.

"Dude!"

"What?"

"I was kinda eavesdropping and everything? And he keeps calling these people and going, 'I've got the next Jewel here. I've got a girl John Mayer.' I mean, Chass, that dude's totally *on*."

"Wow," I said.

"So, Chass," he said, pointing at the floor next to the stage. "Whose beer is that?"

I had forgotten about the beer that the bartender had given me earlier. "You want it?"

"You'd do that for me?"

"Hey," I said. "You're my number one fan."

Number one fan. That's what Ben used to say he was.

I felt a stab of loneliness again as I looked around the room. No Ben. And now he was out with Brittany Arnett. *Once a guy dates a cheerleader, he never goes back to normal girls*—that's what Jay-Jay had said earlier. Was that really true? How had I let him get away?

THIRTY-ONE

EVENTUALLY I HAD played every song that I knew. Some of them twice. My voice was getting hoarse, and most of the kids had started filtering out of Ronnie's. I looked at my watch. Eleven-thirty. Mom should be here in half an hour.

"Okay, guys," I said. "That's about all for tonight. You've been great."

Justin Taylor came up to me immediately and said, "Chass, you mind coming out and sitting in my car for a minute? I'd like to talk."

"Sure." Suddenly I was feeling very nervous. I wanted somebody with me. Mom, Ben—anybody. I felt like, *Who am I kidding? I'm a freakin' sixteen-year-old kid!* But there was no Ben, no Mom. I was going to have to rely on myself.

We walked across the street, and I got in the front seat of a Cadillac Escalade that Justin had parked across the street.

Justin Taylor got in the other side of the car. There was a briefcase on the hump between the seats. He opened it and took out a stack of paper about half an inch thick, held together with a black binder clip.

"You ever seen one of these?" he said.

"What is it?"

He tossed it on my lap.

I read the cover sheet. At the top it said RECORDING CONTRACT in big black letters.

"I carry a blank one in my briefcase wherever I go," he said. "I've been in the music industry for like ten years now, driving around with one of these things, and I've never just handed one to anybody. You know why?"

"Why?"

"Because nobody's that good."

I nodded.

"I mean, I'm empowered to do it. I could fill in all the blanks . . ." He picked up the contract, flipped over a couple of pages, scribbled something on one of the pages, handed it back to me. "See? I can write one zero zero zero zero zero zero on this line, give somebody a contract and, bang, as soon as they sign it, they're an Iambic recording artist with a million-dollar record deal. But, the fact is, in real life you just don't walk up to people on the street and know one hundred percent that this person has the goods to be a star. There's a lot of stuff that has to get sorted out. But in the meantime, I carry this blank contract around and, you know . . . I keep hoping."

We sat in silence, and he picked up the contract.

"You're really an amazing talent, Chass," he said.

"Thanks."

"And you live in this town?"

"Uh-huh."

"Can I get your address?"

I told him the address. He punched it into his Palm Pilot, then scribbled some stuff on the contract.

I could hear his pen scratching on the paper. I wanted so bad for my mom to be there. I wasn't sure what was going on, but I just felt like I was in way over my head. I kept looking over at the entrance to the bar, and Mom kept not being there.

Finally the record company executive flipped the contract shut.

"I saw the way those kids were looking at you. That's

what it's all about. Grabbing kids by the throat, writing the sound track to their lives. I had goose bumps." He tossed the contract in my lap. "There's a first time for everything, Chass."

"Huh?" I said.

"This is a three-album deal. A million bucks for the first album, various escalators, various clauses for the next two albums depending on how the first one does. All you have to do is sign."

I looked at Justin Taylor, my eyes widening, and took a deep breath. I could hear my blood rushing in my ears. This was crazy. He was screwing with me, he had to be.

"Don't sign it now," he said. "Take a few days, think about it, let your lawyers look at it . . ."

My lawyers. Yeah, right.

"Just like that?" I said.

"This is how it happens. One day you're a kid in East Nowhere, Alabama, the next year you're all over the radio. Crazy world, ain't it?" He grinned at me.

He turned to the final page of the contract, pointed at a line that said SIGNATURE next to it.

"Go home, read it, think about it, sleep on it. When you're ready, just sign it right here."

"And that's it."

He nodded. "That's it."

"God." I leaned over and hugged him. "Thank you, thank you, thank you, thank you!"

"Hey, it's nothing."

I put my hand on the door handle, opened the door.

"Oh," he said. "There is one other thing . . ."

And I don't know why, but suddenly my heart fell. Like, here comes the catch.

His smile faded and he reached out his hand. "We'll need the tape."

For a second I didn't know what he was talking about. Then something hit me, like a ghost image on the back of my eyeball. I flipped the contract open and there it was. Right there. Right there above the line where I was supposed to sign, was another blank signature line. Next to the other line were the words: JUSTIN TAYLOR, VICE PRESIDENT OF A&R, IAMBIC RECORDS, A DIVISION OF APEX GLOBAL MEDIA.

Suddenly I felt sick.

"Mr. Van Epps is prepared to make you a star," Justin Taylor said. "I meant every word I just told you. You're crazy talented. You should be out there playing in front of ten thousand people every night. But, baby, the brass ring never comes cheap. You want into the game, you got to give me the tape." He edged closer to me, grabbed hold of my wrist. "Now."

"You bastard," I said. I took the contract, squeezed it into a roll, and slammed it into his face. All rolled up, it was as hard as a piece of wood. He howled and let go of my arm.

I looked at my watch. Four minutes till midnight. Mom was supposed to be here any minute. I got out of the car and started running across the street toward Ronnie's.

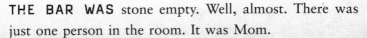

THIRTY-TWO

THE BAR WAS stone empty. Well, almost. There was just one person in the room. It was Mom.

"Mom!" I screamed.

I expected her to look all happy, to run toward me. But she didn't. She just sat there stiffly at a table smack in the middle of the room, staring at me, with her hands flat on the wood. I knew something was wrong. But I ran across the room anyway, yelling, "Mom! Mom!"

And she just kept sitting there, not standing to meet me.

When I reached her, I saw that tears were rolling down her cheeks. And I saw why she didn't stand up. She was attached to the chair with duct tape, loops of it running across her legs, her lap, her stomach.

"I'm sorry, Chass," she said.

"For what?"

"Did you bring the tape?"

I stared at her.

"Answer your mother," a voice said. I recognized it—a fat, smoky voice like an old soul singer or one of those announcers on movie commercials. I turned, and Kyle Van Epps and his two huge goons had risen from behind the bar. The two goons had their pistols pointed at Mom's head.

"My philosophy in life," Van Epps said, "is sometimes you use the carrot, sometimes you use the stick." He walked across the room, sat down next to Mom.

"Please, Chass, sit."

I sat.

"I knew your mom back in the day," he said. "She was amazing. Really a great singer. Great-looking girl. Terrific performer. But you—man!—Chass you've got the whole package. These songs of yours—it's like you're tapping right into the main vein of teenage experience. I could get you on MTV in about eight minutes. I kid you not."

"I don't have the tape," I said.

"It amazes me that people would pass up the opportunity to become rich and famous on some little trivial point of principle. It's perverse. But, you know, hurray for integrity or whatever. Right?"

"Oh, leave her alone, you asshole," Mom said. "Just get it over with."

"Here's my point," Kyle Van Epps said. "I offered you a recording contract for the tape. You stood on principle. Fine. Now, I'm offering not to kill your mom. Either way, you're giving me the tape."

"Don't do it, Chass," Mom said. "Just run."

"Shut up, Jenna," Kyle Van Epps said to her.

"He's gonna kill me either way," Mom said. "He's been hunting us for fifteen years. You think he's just going to let me go?"

"Without the tape, there's nothing," Van Epps said. "I have no need to kill anybody once I get hold of that tape. It's the only evidence that would hold up in court."

"So the e-mail I got today . . ." I said.

"You think I can't afford to hire somebody who can break into some piddling little e-mail account?" Kyle Van Epps laughed pleasantly. "Come on, Chass. Give me some credit. We've been monitoring your e-mail all week. We intercepted your mom's e-mail and then just waited till she showed up."

"Run, Chass," Mom said. "Get away now. Save your-self."

"Where's the tape, Chass?" Mr. Van Epps said.

I sighed loudly. "I'll go get it."

"Good," Mr. Van Epps said. "Frank and I will come with you. Carlos will stay here with Mommy."

Mr. Van Epps and I stood and walked toward the door. One of the big stooges followed. He opened the door of a yellow Hummer sitting at the curb.

"Where to?" Kyle Van Epps said.

I pointed. "That way."

The big guy named Frank started driving, and I gave directions until we reached the old cotton mill. After a couple of minutes it loomed up over us, the biggest build-ing in town, a dark and forbidding shadow against the night sky.

"Well?" Kyle Van Epps said when we pulled up in front of the mill.

"It's inside," I said. "But before I get it for you, I have some questions to ask."

"Sorry, babe," he said, "but it doesn't work like that."

"Sure it does," I said. "You've been harassing me and my mom for sixteen years. You can wait another five minutes."

Mr. Van Epps laughed, then looked at his watch. "All right, what. You got five minutes."

"Why is this so important to you?"

"Uh, you listened to the tape, right?"

"Sure."

"So you know that Jimmy Laws alleges that I killed this girl." He flashed me a cynical smile. "Which, of course, I did not do."

"I'm sure."

"Whether it's true or not, if this tape reached the right people, I could be indicted, dragged through the mud. It would be a very big problem for me. Even if I never got convicted."

"And you've been chasing us all this time."

"I've had people on it, sure."

"So when Mom made me pack up and leave all my friends, it wasn't because she was crazy or paranoid."

"We had some close calls, times we almost got her, yeah."

I sat there silently for a minute.

"All right, enough stalling," Kyle Van Epps said.

"Just one more question," I said. "Who is Edward Wong working for?"

"What?"

"Edward Wong. I thought he was working for you."

Mr. Van Epps's eyes narrowed. "Are you saying Wong is *here*?"

I nodded. "Sure."

His face hardened. "Son of a—" He flipped open his cell, hit a speed-dial number. "Wong's in town," he shouted into the phone. "You need to get Jenna in the car. Now. If Wong shows up, do what you have to do to Jenna."

Jenna. It was hard to get used to the notion that Mom's real name was Jenna.

Mr. Van Epps grabbed my wrist so hard I winced. "Let's go," he said.

I got out of the car, Mr. Van Epps still holding on to my wrist. Frank, Mr. Van Epps's thug, was following after us with his gun out.

"It's back here," I said. The cotton mill was about seventy-five years old. It had been shut down a long time ago. There was a rusty old chain-link fence surrounding the property, but most of the kids in town knew where the holes in the fence were. The place was spooky at night, with old pieces of rusting equipment looming in the dark, broken windows staring out like vacant eyes. I felt a terrible sense of foreboding as we made our way toward the fence.

I knew that Mom was probably right. Once he had the tape, Mr. Van Epps would likely kill Mom and me both. I had to do something in a hurry.

We walked through a broken door and into the interior of the old building. It had once been three stories tall, but the top two floors had collapsed, so you could see all the way up to the roof, fifty feet above us. The building was about two hundred feet long. You had to walk carefully, because the bottom floor had fallen through in a couple of places, and if you weren't looking where you were going, you'd fall right through into the basement.

"Give me your phone," I said to Mr. Van Epps.

"Yeah, right."

"Look," I said, "this is a big place. There are a lot of places I could have hidden that tape. I'm not showing it to you until I can be sure that Mom's okay."

Van Epps took out a gun and pointed it at my head. "How about this? How about I just kill you right now?"

"What good would that do you? You think I haven't told anybody where I put the tape?"

"I'm sure that will be a big consolation to you while you're lying here dead on the ground."

I shrugged, then crossed my arms and stopped walking. I was terrified. But at the same time I knew that if I let Van Epps know how scared I was, Mom and I were dead. "So we're kind of at a standoff," I said.

"Punch her in the face," Van Epps said to his bodyguard, Frank.

"Look, you can beat on me for a while, see how quick

I agree to help you," I said. "But every minute you spend here is a minute that Wong is catching up to you. Just put Mom on the phone."

Van Epps studied my face, then hit his speed dial. "Put Jenna on, Carlos," he said. Then he handed me the phone.

"Mom?" I said.

"Hey, sweetheart." Her voice sounded heavy and dull.

"Where are you?"

"In a car, driving around."

"Tell the guy you're with to drive you to the sheriff's department. Pull up in front of the station and park."

I could hear her talking to Mr. Van Epps's thug.

I handed the phone to Van Epps. "Explain it to your boy, Carlos."

Mr. Van Epps did what I told him to. "But don't let her out of the car!" he snapped. Then he handed the phone back to me.

"Okay, they're parked in front of the sheriff's office. Now get that tape."

I walked across the big, dark, echoing space, stopped near the loose brick where the tape was stored. "When I hand you the tape, you tell your guy to push her out of the car," I said.

"All right." Mr. Van Epps held the phone to his ear. "Where's the tape?"

"Over here."

"I assume you made copies," Van Epps said.

"Mom may have, but I didn't," I said.

"Well, it won't matter, from a legal perspective. Copies of some ancient tape made by a dead man would never be admissible in court. Only the original would make it into court."

I put my hand on the brick, pulled it out. "Here it is," I said.

Mr. Van Epps reached into the hole then came out with the tape. He handed it to his henchman Frank, who scrutinized it carefully, then nodded.

"That's the one," Frank said. "The serial number's right and everything."

"Good," Van Epps said. Then he spoke into the phone. "Kill Jenna, Carlos," he said. There was obviously some protest from his man on the other end of the line. "I don't care if you're ten feet from the sheriff's department or not. Kill her."

So much for my brilliant plan. I felt sick.

He took the tape from his stooge and started walking back to the car. Over his shoulder he said, "Take care of her, Frank."

I started running. It was the only thing I could do. The big man, Frank, pursued me. He was a young athletic guy, and I could see he'd catch me soon. The one advantage I had was that I had been here in the dark before and he hadn't.

I dodged through the maze of old equipment. I could hear him breathing heavily behind me. I charged across the old building, then took a sudden turn to the right. Yawning below me was a huge black hole in the ground, where the floor had caved into a basement. I edged onto a small catwalk, the remnant of an old support beam, that swayed uneasily across the yawning hole.

I stood for a moment, considering whether or not I should jump down into the inky darkness. I knew there was a back door from the basement out into the river. The question was, would I kill myself jumping down into the dark.

Before I had made my decision, Frank burst out from behind an old loom and hurled himself toward me.

There was a brief moment when a moonbeam caught his face. I could see the surprise and fear on his face, his eyes going wide as he realized there was no floor below him. Then he was just a black shape falling into a blacker hole.

There was a thud and a crack, like a sack of coconuts being dropped on a hard floor. Then, nothing.

My heart pounded as I waited to see if Frank was going to move again. He might be waiting down there, trying to get a shot at me. If I moved, he'd see me.

So I stood there motionless, balancing on the rickety old beam for what seemed like an hour. Finally I decided that I had to go. I began making my way slowly, slowly back across the beam. Still nothing from below.

I regained some sense of hope. I made my way slowly, quietly through the wrecked building and out into the moonlight. About a hundred feet away I could see Kyle Van Epps. He had made a small fire out of trash and was about to throw the tape into it. His face looked eerie in the flickering light. I could see the tape in his hand. He was smiling like some kind of huge weight was coming off his shoulders.

If the tape went in the fire, I was out of leverage.

"Hey!" I called.

He looked over at me, startled.

"Where's Frank?" he said.

"Dead, I think," I said.

He frowned, then shrugged. "Well, that's a shame for him, huh?" Then he threw the tape in the fire. My stomach sank as the flames licked up around the edges of the tape reel.

He pulled out his pistol and pointed it at me. Then he began backing away from the fire.

"You can run," he said. "But of course without the tape, you're sunk. So here's what I'm going to do. You can try and get the tape out of the fire. It actually takes a while to burn an entire tape. You might be able to save the relevant portion. I'm not the world's best shot, I'll be honest. There's a chance you might be able to get it out and then outrun me. I'm overweight and out of shape. You might get out of this alive." His teeth gleamed in the light. He was now about thirty feet from the fire. "Then again you might not. But you better hurry or the tape will be gone."

I didn't see that I had any choice. I sprinted toward the tape, pulled it out of the fire. The reel had melted a little, but the tape itself was still more or less intact. I shrieked as the molten plastic burned itself into my skin. In that moment of shock, I hurled the reel of tape to the ground.

And by then, Mr. Van Epps had gotten to within five or ten feet of me. The gun was pointed right at my chest.

"Nice try," he said. He shook his head sadly. We both stared down at the reel of tape, smoldering on the ground between us.

"What a waste. You should have just signed the contract," he said. "You could have been huge."

"Yeah, well, look at you," I said. "You're huge and you're *still* a waste."

He laughed briefly, then sighed. "I really hate killing you," he said. "But a man's gotta do what a man's gotta do."

He bent over, picked up the tape with a soft grunt, then pointed his gun at my face.

"See you in the next life, Chass."

"I don't think so," a voice said.

I turned, and there was a tall, thin figure rising up from behind Mr. Van Epps.

I stared.

"Ben?" I said finally.

The tall, thin figure raised a rusty steel pipe and swung it at Van Epps. But Van Epps was quicker than he looked. He stepped back, evading the pipe, pivoted the gun around toward Ben. Without thinking, I slammed into him as hard as I could. Mr. Van Epps stumbled and fell into the small bonfire he'd just built. He was up as quickly as he'd gone down, but now his coat was on fire. He swatted at the fire with his hands, his eyes full of terror.

"Put it out! Put it out!" he screamed, thrashing wildly at his clothes.

But Ben and I just stepped back and watched.

He kept slapping at his clothes and jumping around like a crazy man. Suddenly there was a loud bang. Van Epps turned and looked at me, his body gone motionless. The fire on his clothes was out now, just a trace of smoke rising up off the blackened lapel of his fancy suit. Then he dropped to his knees. There was a hole in the side of his face, and blood was flowing out faster than I imagined was possible. His gun must have gone off as he was slapping at the fire.

He reached for the tape, scrabbling feebly on the ground. Then he fell over on top of it and didn't move.

Ben ran over, grabbed me, and wrapped his arms around me.

"Ben!" I said. "But . . . I thought . . ."

"What?" he murmured.

"I thought you and Brittany . . ."

"Brittany?" he said. "Who's Brittany?"

I wanted to ask more questions, to find out how he had gotten here. But suddenly something hit me. "Oh my God," I said.

I grabbed Ben's hand and started sprinting toward the road. I could see the Batmobile parked up near Mr. Van Epps's car.

"We've got to get to Mom before he kills her!"

THIRTY-THREE

WHEN WE REACHED downtown, there were a bunch of sheriff's cars and ambulances circled up in the middle of Main Street. All the emergency vehicles had their lights flashing, giving the downtown the look of some weird carnival. In the middle of the big circle of cars lay a human figure, covered by a bloodstained sheet. Sheriff Arnett was standing nearby, talking on his cell phone.

I ran up screaming, "No! No! Mom! No!"

The sheriff grabbed me as I tried to reach the figure on the ground.

"Don't," he said. "Don't."

I had never felt so horrible, so lost in my life. The strength went out of my legs, and I sagged against Sheriff Arnett.

But then something miraculous happened.

As he grabbed me, Mom stepped out from behind an ambulance and grinned. She ran toward me. We slammed into each other like a couple of football players. I hugged her and hugged her. It seemed like I couldn't let go.

Five minutes later, we were seated in the lobby of the sheriff's office. "Chass, meet Edward Wong," Mom said.

"We've met," I said. But I shook his hand anyway.

Edward Wong was sitting across from us, his face expressionless.

"So who is he?" I said to Mom.

Wong answered for himself. "I used to be a New York cop."

"Yeah, but why are you here?"

"I guess you could say I have a grudge against Kyle Van Epps."

I frowned curiously at him. "Why?"

"I was the investigating detective in the disappearance of Angelica Robinson. I was sure that Van Epps had something to do with it. I kept pushing, and finally Jimmy Laws called me and said he was going to tell me what happened. Next thing I knew, there was this tragic boating accident, and Jimmy was dead. When I tried to keep the investigation alive, Kyle Van Epps decided he needed to get me out of the way. So he set me up. He made it look like I was taking bribes. I got kicked off the force and ended up out in L.A. I went to law school, hated being a lawyer, ended up doing private investigation work. As you might imagine, I was pretty angry at Kyle Van Epps. So I've been pursuing the Angelica Robinson case in my spare time all these years."

"But what about Niles Henry? He had Mr. Van Epps's number on his phone. We called Mr. Van Epps, and he obviously knew who Niles Henry was."

"Niles was an operative of mine. I sent him out here to follow up on a lead that indicated your mother might be out here. He obviously figured out more about the case than I had told him. And once he did that, Niles realized the information about your mother was worth lots of money to Van Epps. So he sold me out to Kyle."

I turned to Mom. I didn't say anything. And for a minute, neither did she. But there must have been something in my eyes, something accusing, because suddenly she looked away from me.

"I was just trying to protect you," she said finally.

"I never had a name," I said. "I never knew anything."

"I know, I know," she said. "After Jimmy was killed,

Kyle came to me and he said, 'I know about the tape. Give it to me.' He threatened to kill me if I didn't. By that time, I was already soured on the music business. I hated touring, I hated the money problems, I hated the jerks at the record companies and the managers who ripped you off and the club owners who refused to pay and the fans who loved you one day and hated you the next. And I just . . . I just felt like I had to escape.

"So I took you and the tape, and I hit the road, drove out to Chicago. At first I thought it would all be over after a little while. But then some thugs that Kyle had hired caught up with me. They didn't have any trouble finding me. I was using a fake name, but I was playing in clubs. I guess it wasn't hard to find out about me through the musical grapevine. So they showed up one night after I got home from a gig. They . . ." Mom's face darkened. "They came into our apartment, and they picked you up, and they held you out a window by one leg. You were only about three months old at the time. I thought you were dead. My brother had given me a pistol. I pulled it out and said, 'If you drop my baby, I kill you both.' They let you go, and we got away. But I made a vow that I'd never put you in that position again. So I said to myself, after this I'll be careful. I'll never speak my real name, and I'll never have anything to do with music. I mean, I love music so much . . ." Her eyes looked haunted. "Any time I heard music, it was like Kyle Van Epps was personally taunting me, telling me about a life I could never live again. So I just . . . I just cut it out of my life. It was too painful."

That explained a lot. I went over and hugged her, then said, "So what happened the night you disappeared, Mom?"

"I was feeling so strange. Because I heard you playing, and I just knew." Her eyes brimmed with tears. "I just knew that this was your destiny. And I had spent your whole life trying to take it away from you. I felt terrible. So I drove around for a while. While I was driving, I got this weird call. This guy tells me that his name is Niles Henry, that he's working for Edward Wong, that he's here to help. Any other time, I'd have gone straight home, packed you in the car, and hit the road. But right then? Feeling the way I did? I just thought, well, maybe this is my chance to fix this thing. So I met him at McDonald's, told him that I had come here three years ago to try and piece together part of the story that Jimmy had told me, the part about Nancy Rydel. I told him that it would be verification that what he was saying on the tape was true. I told him I'd been trying to build a case against Kyle Van Epps for years, something that would be unsinkable, so we could come out of hiding for good."

"That's what all the fake ID cards were for?" I said. "The ones for all those companies that were part of Apex Global Media?"

"Right. So I made a decision on the spot. I'd have to trust him. Bad decision, in retrospect. Anyway, I told Niles that I'd show him where I believed that Nancy Rydel was buried. We drove over there, got out of the car, and went down into the basement. Once we were down there, he started pushing me to tell him where the tape was. I immediately got suspicious. There were some old knives and things on the walls, so I grabbed one when he wasn't looking. He knocked a couple bricks out of the wall where Nancy was buried while I was stalling about telling him where the tape was. Then I guess he finally got the picture, because he turned around and said if I didn't tell him where the tape was, he'd kill me. I managed to stick him with the knife and get out of the cellar. Then I ran off into the darkness and got away from him.

"After that, I figured that he'd go straight back to our apartment. If I went back there, he'd kill us both. So I hid in the woods, then hitched a ride up to Birmingham, where I could lay low for a couple of days until I could come back and get you. Anyway, I arranged for the ad in the paper from up there, the one that told you how to find the tape in the bank. I didn't want to call because I was afraid Kyle might be tracking our phones. My plan was to contact you once you got the tape, and then we'd hit the road immediately. But unfortunately Kyle Van Epps spotted me when I came back into town and grabbed me and . . ." She smiled without humor. "Well, you know the rest."

I turned to Ben. "What about you? I thought you hated me now. I thought you and Brittany were going to the movies or something."

He shrugged. "We had a fight. I told her I wasn't gonna miss your show. I mean, yeah, I'm mad about my dad and everything. But still. I just felt like I had to see you at your first gig. When I told that to Brittany, she told me to go to hell. She said I was your lapdog or something like that. So I drove over to Ronnie's, and then I was like, man, I'll look like such a loser if I go slinking in there with my tail between my legs." He smiled ruefully. "So I sat on the Dumpster out back and listened to the whole thing through the window."

"Are you serious?" I said. "That is so sweet. In a really pathetic, twisted way, I mean."

Everybody laughed. Ben took my hand. I felt that *ksshhhh ksshhhh* thing happening again. It almost made me dizzy.

"So I'm sitting out there afterward," he said. "I was gonna wait till it was over and then come and apologize for going off with Brittany, but then while I'm sitting in the parking lot, making up my mind, I see this bunch of dudes show up with your mom. And one of them's got this gun jammed up under her arm. I was going to go to the sheriff, but then these guys drive off with you in the car, and I'm like, if I don't follow you, you're screwed. So I followed you down to the mill."

I frowned. "What about you, Mom?" I said. "Mr. Van Epps told that guy Carlos to kill you. What happened?"

"I was staking out the downtown area," Edward Wong said. "I just happened to be in the right place at the right time. If you hadn't done what you did, Chass, your mom would be dead now. Anyway, I saw your mom in there with that big ape of a guy. I figured I'd sort of sit on the situation, see what developed. Suddenly your mom's trying to get out of the car, and the big guy is pointing a pistol at her. I just hopped out of my truck, unholstered my piece, and . . ." He hesitated. "Well, now Van Epps's guy is lying on the ground under a sheet."

We sat in silence for a moment.

"So is it true?" I said finally. "Is Jimmy Laws my father?"

Mom looked at me curiously. "Jimmy *Laws*? That little snake? God no! What gave you that impression?"

"The blond hair, the musical talent, the snub nose . . ." I told her about the picture in the magazine, Jimmy with his arm around her.

She laughed. "We were just taking a bow at the end of the show. I couldn't stand the guy."

"So . . ." I hesitated. "So who *is* my father?"

"His name was Nick Farmer. He was a recording engineer. We fell in love and got married while I was recording my first album. He worked for Kyle. He was the one who recorded the tape of Jimmy's confession. We were sitting around the studio when Jimmy came in. I was working on a track, and Jimmy interrupted. Jimmy had been drinking. Your father just kept the recording equipment rolling, and that's how it ended up on tape."

My eyes widened.

Mom paused for a minute.

"Two men died on Kyle Van Epps's boat that night," she said finally. "Your father was the second man."

I started to cry.

"Kyle killed him because he made the tape."

Sheriff Arnett had been listening to the whole thing. He turned to Ben and said, "You know what, son? Given what I've heard just now—as well as a few things that Mr. Wong and Ms. Pureheart told me before y'all got here, I think it's time we let your father out of jail. It's obvious he didn't kill Nancy Rydel."

He waved to one of his deputies, who led Mr. Purvis out from inside the sheriff's office. He and Ben gave each other a big hug.

"Of course, just for confirmation, I will need to listen to that tape," the sheriff said.

My eyes widened.

"What is it, Bugaboo?" Mom said.

I stood and started running toward the door. "The tape! We forgot the tape!"

THIRTY-FOUR

MOM AND I rode in the backseat of Sheriff Arnett's car to the old mill. Three sheriff's cruisers followed, their lights flashing.

"Wait!" I yelled. "There!"

Off the road to our left I could see the dark shape of Mr. Van Epps's Hummer. Something was moving beside the big truck. It looked like Frank, the big thug who had chased me through the mill. He must have survived his fall into the basement of the mill and then pulled the Hummer down the hill close to the fence around the mill.

He was hunched over, doing something next to the open rear door of the truck.

The sheriff veered sharply off the road, jumped out of the car.

"Y'all two stay here," he said sternly to me and Mom.

"Yes, sir," I said. But as soon as he turned away and began to run toward the Hummer, I opened the door.

"Chass!" Mom hissed. "You get back here this minute."

"I have to get the tape," I said.

"Chass!"

I followed the sheriff down the little hill toward the fence surrounding the mill. Hearing us, Frank whirled. There was a gun in his hand. I could see Kyle Van Epps lying on the backseat. Frank must have been loading his boss into the back to drive away with him.

I saw the hole in the fence, ran through it. As my eyes adjusted to the dimness, I spotted a couple of embers glowing on the ground. The remains of Kyle Van Epps's fire. I ran toward them.

Behind me I heard gunshots.

"There's six of us and one of you!" yelled the sheriff to Frank. "Don't be a fool."

Frank answered him with a burst of gunfire.

I scanned the ground. There it was! The tape. I scooped it up, slid it into the waistband of my pants, pulled my T-shirt out so it covered the tape.

As I was getting ready to head back toward the sheriff's car, I heard the door of the Hummer slam, then something crashed into the fence about fifty feet away from me. I looked toward the Hummer, saw Frank leap onto the fence. He may have been big, but he wasn't clumsy. He scaled the high fence in a heartbeat, leapt over, and was dodging through the darkness before the sheriff's men could do anything to stop him. I could hear him moving stealthily through the collection of junk outside the mill, finding cover so the sheriff's men couldn't shoot him.

I ducked behind an old piece of textile machinery. For a moment everything was silent. Then I heard footsteps moving quietly toward me. What if Frank found me? I tried to hide by huddling into the machine, but there really was no place to go. There were some boards on the ground. Worst-case scenario, maybe I could whack him with one. I grabbed the nearest two-by-four with both hands, pulled it toward me.

"I see him!" one of the sheriff's men yelled.

"Over there!" Sheriff Arnett yelled.

Frank began running. His footsteps grew closer and closer.

"He's getting away!" a voice yelled.

Through a crack in the machine I could see a couple of deputies trying to scale the fence—but they were both overweight, scared-looking guys—no match for Frank in the fence-climbing department. I figured if Frank made it to the river on the other side of the mill, he'd get away. All he'd have to do was swim downriver a few hundred yards, cross to the other bank, and he'd be off into the state forest, where the sheriff and his men would never find him.

The footsteps pounded closer and closer. He was going to pass right in front of me.

My first impulse was to huddle as deep in the shadows as I could. But at the last second, I changed my mind. I shoved the board out in front of me, right at knee level.

In the darkness, Frank never saw it. His shin hit the wood, which splintered on impact. Frank tripped and smashed to the ground. Something metallic clanged. In a shaft of moonlight I could make out Frank on the ground, holding his knee and moaning. Behind him, on the ground, lay his gun. I jumped up, ran around him, and made a grab for the gun.

Just as my fingers closed on the grip of the pistol, Frank's fingers wrapped around my ankles.

"I'm gonna kill you this time, girl," he said.

I swung the gun around, pointed it at his head. "Go ahead," I said. "Try it."

His black eyes stared at me for a long time. Finally

his grip released on my leg. I stepped back, still pointing the gun at the big man on the ground.

"Over here," I yelled.

A couple of deputies arrived seconds later, huffing and puffing, followed by Sheriff Arnett.

"Put the gun down, Chass," the sheriff said. "We got everything under control now."

"I believe that little gal's the one got things under control, boss," one of the deputies said, grinning. The other deputy laughed loudly.

The sheriff narrowed his eyes at the two deputies, and they abruptly stopped laughing.

"One of you comedians cuff this boy," the sheriff said.

I handed the sheriff Frank's gun, then walked slowly back toward the fence. Nobody seemed to notice me. I crawled through the hole, went back up to the sheriff's car, where Mom was standing.

"You are grounded for the rest of your life, young lady," she said hotly. "Do not *ever* do that to me again. You could have been killed."

I looked around to see if anybody was paying attention to us, then I lifted up the hem of my shirt so she could see the tape that I'd stuffed down my pants.

Mom's face slowly relaxed, then she shook her head, trying unsuccessfully to stifle a grin.

"Do we want to give this to Sheriff Arnett or not?" I said. "I mean don't you think it might be safer to give it to the FBI or something?"

Mom nodded, suddenly looking serious. "That's a very good question," she said.

We stood together by the sheriff's car for a while. Eventually an ambulance came and picked up Kyle Van Epps. It was obvious from the swiftness with which the EMTs got him in the ambulance and whisked him away—siren blaring and lights flashing, two heavily armed deputies sitting in the back—that Kyle Van Epps wasn't dead yet. I wasn't sure if I felt good about that or not.

It was silent for a while, the deputies milling around below us, looking all puffed up with the success of their big bust. No one seemed to be paying any attention to us at all.

"So what do you think?" Mom said.

"About what?"

"Where should we go next? We can go anywhere, you know."

I looked around. A few lights from downtown High Hopes glimmered way off in the darkness. I knew Ben was over there somewhere. This was as close to being home as anyplace I'd ever lived.

"I think," I said, "I'd like to stay here."

"What about your name?" Mom said. "Your real name is—"

"Yeah," I said. "I know what my real name is. Darcy Farmer. Kyle Van Epps told me."

Mom winced. "It should have been me," she said. "I should have been the one to tell you, . . . Darcy."

"You did fine, Mom," I said. I gave her a squeeze. "Anyway, what's the big deal? I don't really think I'm a Darcy anyway."

"Then what should I call you?"

It took me a minute but suddenly I knew. Something lifted inside me, like a kite taking off into the sky. I smiled as I spoke it out loud—my own name, my real name, the name of the person I chose to be:

"Chass," I said. "My name's Chass."

Turn the page for a sneak preview
of Chastity's next adventure,

CLUB DREAD

ONE

I WAS TAPING a blue piece of photocopied paper to the window of this coffeehouse called Java Monkey when a guy walked up behind me. He looked over my shoulder at the poster and then read it out loud in this kind of snotty voice.

"FEMALE SINGER-SONGWRITER LOOKING FOR BAND. BASS PLAYER, DRUMMER, KEYS NEEDED. SERIOUS PRO PLAYERS ONLY. CALL CHASS AT 415-555-2783."

I glared at him.

"You're not gonna find anybody this way," he said.

"Excuse me?" I said. "Do I know you?"

"What you'll get is losers. No serious professional musician would answer an ad like this. Plus, if they did?" He looked me up and down. "Who'd want to be in a band led by some fifteen-year-old girl?"

"First," I said, "I happen to be sixteen. And second, who made you the big expert?"

He just smirked at me.

Which was when I noticed it was Josh Emmit. *The* Josh Emmit. The Josh Emmit with the show on MTV, the Josh Emmit with all the hit records, the Josh Emmit with the line of sneakers that every girl in eighth grade is wearing this year—*that* Josh Emmit. I like to think I'm not one of these dopey girls that flips out and gets all peeing in their pants and screaming when they see somebody famous. But still. I mean it *was* Josh Emmit. I just stared at him like a moron, my mouth hanging open.

Then there was this loud pop from the road, and Josh Emmit was like, "Ow! That hurt."

Then there was another pop. Really loud.

For a second I thought maybe somebody had thrown some firecrackers at him. He had this funny look on his face, like somebody had said something to him that didn't make any sense. Then he grabbed his stomach and kind of hunched over against the wall, and all this blood started leaking out between his fingers.

I started screaming. "Oh my God, somebody just shot Josh Emmit! Oh my God, somebody just shot Josh Emmit!"

But there was nobody on the street to hear me. Nobody, that is, except the guy in the front seat of the big red car that was heading off down the road away from us. Josh grabbed my hand and he goes, "Hey. Hey, kid. Take this."

I looked at the thing he was handing me. It looked like a little bar of silver. It was very heavy. The number 53 was stamped into it. I turned it over; the number 100 was stamped on the other side.

"Take it and get out of here. Before they find you."

I stopped screaming long enough to say, "Before *who* finds me?"

Down the street, the red car threw on its brakes with a loud screech. The taillights went on and the car began to back up.

Little red bubbles had started coming out of Josh Emmit's mouth, and he was making this weird noise like when you suck on a milk-shake straw after the milk shake is all gone. He was trying to say something.

"What?" I said.

He pulled me toward him. "Stop. Stop . . . the hundred," he said in this bubbly, feeble voice. He waved his hand toward the road. I could see the skyline of San Francisco down the road in the direction he was pointing. The big red car was still backing toward us, getting closer and closer. I could see sunglasses reflected in the side-view mirror.

"Huh?" I said.

"Hundred. Stop. Hundred."

"A hundred what?"

"Promise me."

The car was getting closer and closer. "I would promise if I understood you, but I just—"

Josh Emmit looked over at the car, then pressed his hand against mine, folding my fingers around the silver ingot. The car was not more than thirty yards away, closing fast. "Go," he said. "Now!"

He didn't have to tell me twice. Believe me, I know all about running for your life. So that's what I did.

Okay, so I'm only sixteen years old. That doesn't mean I'm a total dumb ass. I figured if somebody had just shot Josh Emmit for whatever it was that I was carrying in my hand, this little ingot thing, then they'd probably do something even worse to me. So after about half a block, I took this thing that he'd given me and tried to chunk it into a Dumpster. I'm not like Little Miss Future Olympic Softball Champion, so this ingot thing missed, banked off the Dumpster with this huge clang, and fell behind some boxes.

I did *not* stop to pick it up and try throwing it in the Dumpster again.

I just kept running.

TWO

WHEN I GOT home, I went in my room, took out my guitar, and played until Mom came home from work. She's a waitress, working the dinner shift, so it was kind of late by the time she showed up.

She poked her head in my room and said, "How was your day, sweetie?"

And I said, "Fine."

"Did you do your homework?"

"Yeah," I lied.

She looked at me with this funny expression on her face. "Are you okay, Chass?"

"*Fine!*" I said. The word came out a little sharp. "I'm just tired is all. I think I'm going to bed."

Mom narrowed her eyes slightly. I got up before she could start doing the parental third degree, went to my bed, and lay down for a while. I couldn't sleep. Then I got back up and went into the living room, where Mom was reading a book.

Mom looked up at me, raised one eyebrow.

"Actually?" I said.

Mom waited.

"Actually, something did happen."

After I'd explained about Josh Emmit, she said, "This is not good. This is really not good."

"I didn't know what to do," I said. "I just ran. Should I have called the police?"

She looked at me for a long time, then finally, in a very quiet voice said, "No. No, honey, you did the right thing."

It's kind of a long story—why not calling the police was the right thing. What it comes down to is that Mom and I have been on the run for a long time. Mom has information about a murder committed by a very powerful man named Kyle Van Epps, and for my entire life Van Epps has been trying to catch up with us. Every now and then, he gets close to us. When that happens we have to change our names and move to a new town on about half an hour's notice. We thought we had gotten it all worked out a few months back, but then things went bad, and we had to run again.

What happened was that Van Epps had been charged with a murder in Alabama. At the time he had been shot and was in the hospital. But while he was recuperating, his minions managed to pay off some police, intimidate some witnesses, and generally make the case against him go away. At a certain point it became clear we had to grab the tape and run again—or he'd make us go away too.

"If we had any kind of a normal life," Mom said, "going to the police would be the only right thing to do. But if you go talk to them and they start running us through the computer, they'll find that we just sprang into existence about a month ago."

"I know, I know . . ."

"I realize how hard it was for you to leave Alabama, to leave Ben. I don't want to have to do that to you again."

Ben was my sort-of boyfriend in the last town where we had lived. I sat there glumly and nodded.

"Turn on the news," Mom said. "Let's see if there's anything about it."

We were about to flip on the TV when the doorbell rang. Mom's eyes darted toward the door. It was eleven o'clock at night. You didn't usually have visitors at that hour. She went over and looked out the peephole.

"Who is it?"

"Police, ma'am. I'm looking for someone named Chass."

"Slide your ID under the door, please," Mom said.

There was a pause, then a scratchy sound. A police ID appeared from under the door.

"Somebody must have seen me at the coffeehouse," I said. My heart was racing. "What are we gonna do?"

Mom took a deep breath. "We'll let him in," Mom said softly. "Just tell him what you saw. Don't give any details. Skip the part about Josh Emmit giving you whatever it was he gave you. Just say you were putting up the poster, he walked by and got shot. You were afraid and you ran."

I nodded.

"Keep it soft focus." Mom unlocked the door, looked out through the crack. "What is it?" she said through the door.

"Inspector Jerry Wise, San Francisco Police Department. Are you Chass?"

"That's my daughter's nickname. Why?"

"I need to speak to her about a homicide that occurred this afternoon."

"Come on in," Mom said.

The inspector was a chubby little guy with a red, watchful face. He wore a suit and bright red suspenders. "Chass?" he said, holding up the blue poster I'd left on the wall of the coffeehouse that afternoon.

"I should have called," I said. "I was just . . . I was just really scared."

The inspector took out a small notepad. "You were just scared. I see. Well, how about you get unscared long enough to come down to the station and talk to me."

I looked at Mom.

"What's wrong with talking here?" Mom said.

The inspector turned his sour little eyes toward Mom. "What's wrong is, I didn't ask if she wanted to talk here."

"Well, I'm asking," Mom said. "It's eleven o'clock at night. She has to go to school in the morning."

"And this seems to you like a bigger consideration than the fact that a young man was murdered this afternoon? No, I want her down at the station."

I could see Mom thinking about it. Finally I think she decided we would end up being better off not making a scene.